"You said you wouldn't let me get away from you," Leah said, *"but I did get away. At least for a little while."*

"You weren't free of me a moment. I was with you all night. Just like you were with me." With a quickness that stunned her, he rounded her desk and hauled her into his arms. "Do you know why we had no peace? Because we needed desperately to be together."

The kiss came as no surprise to her. Neither did the fact that desire flamed up in her so quickly she was left weak.

He'd never known a woman as responsive, and it excited him as nothing ever had. The nerves just beneath her skin were charged with currents of fire and emotion. "Tell me you couldn't get away from me last night," he demanded. He pressed kisses all over her face. "Tell me I was crawling through your bloodstream, just like you were through mine."

She gave a little cry. "Yes, oh, yes." As he pressed his mouth to hers once more, her mind was lost in clouds and fire. . . .

WHAT ARE *LOVESWEPT* ROMANCES?

They are stories of true romance and touching emotion. We believe those two very important ingredients are constants in our highly sensual and very believable stories in the *LOVESWEPT* line. Our goal is to give you, the reader, stories of consistently high quality that may sometimes make you laugh, sometimes make you cry, but are always fresh and creative and contain many delightful surprises within their pages.

Most romance fans read an enormous number of books. Those they truly love, they keep. Others may be traded with friends and soon forgotten. We hope that each *LOVESWEPT* romance will be a treasure—a "keeper." We will always try to publish

LOVE STORIES YOU'LL NEVER FORGET
BY AUTHORS YOU'LL ALWAYS REMEMBER

The Editors

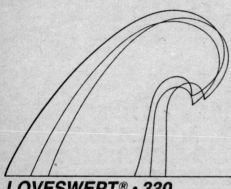

LOVESWEPT® · 330

Fayrene Preston

The Pearls of

Sharah III:

Leah's Story

 BANTAM BOOKS
NEW YORK · TORONTO · LONDON · SYDNEY · AUCKLAND

THE PEARLS OF SHARAH III:
LEAH'S STORY

A Bantam Book / June 1989

If you would be interested in receiving protective vinyl
covers for your Loveswept books, please write to this address
for information:

Loveswept
Bantam Books
P.O. Box 985
Hicksville, NY 11802

ISBN 0-553-21993-6

Published simultaneously in the United States and Canada

Bantam Books are published by Bantam Books, a division
of Bantam Doubleday Dell Publishing Group, Inc. Its trade-
mark, consisting of the words "Bantam Books" and the
portrayal of a rooster, is Registered in U.S. Patent and
Trademark Office and in other countries. Marca Registrada.
Bantam Books, 666 Fifth Avenue, New York, New York 10103.

The Pearls of Sharah series
is dedicated with all my love
to my sons,

Greg and Jeff,

two very special people.

Prologue

Persepolis
515 B.C.

Far beneath the surface of the swelling waves, in the dark, mysterious, primordial depths of the sea, the pearls grew and waited.

Until . . .

King Darius was coming.

Princess Sharah sat by a pool of still water while a handmaiden ran a comb through the shimmering length of her black hair. Lotus blossoms floated on the pool that reflected the princess's serenely beautiful face. But just as the deep water hid the dark roots of the blossoms, so, too, did her serene countenance hide troubled thoughts.

With a wave of her hand she dismissed the

handmaiden. None of the servants had yet sensed their lord's approach, but Sharah did not need to see him or even to hear the soft tread of his footsteps to know he was near. She did not require Darius's presence to feel his every breath. She could not explain why this was, nor did she need to. She was a princess of the Karzana, a nomadic tribe, and she accepted that there were powers which could not be understood.

All she needed to know was that her blood sang when he strode through the halls of the great palace toward her private rooms here in the tower, and that the very air around her seemed to fill with excitement.

There was a stirring among her handmaidens. One of them tittered, then another. Ah, now they also knew he was coming.

Darius was drawing close.

On those nights when Darius came to her bed-chamber, she accepted his attentions because circumstances had forced her to do so. She also writhed in pleasure beneath him, because he was a lover of great accomplishment. And afterward she held him through the night until dawn because, secreted within her heart, was a profound and deep love for him.

But she was also proud, and she refused to surrender her soul to him as he was determined she would. . . .

With the power of a great wind Darius strode into the chamber and clapped his hands. "Leave us."

The serving girls bowed and dispersed.

Sharah lifted her head and gazed at him. Every line of his strong body bespoke command and power. Even without the royal robes he wore he would have looked kingly. Nevertheless, his *candy* was of bluish-purple; his sash was of cloth of gold; and his shawl was ornamented with rubies, emeralds, sapphires, and diamonds.

The gods had bestowed all the manly graces on Darius, Sharah thought once again, and she knew that hearts beat fast within the breasts of all the fair young women upon whom he deigned to look.

But it was only she he wanted. And so she waited.

He held out his hand to her. "Come here, my love."

The dark blue silk of her full trousers and tunic murmured as she rose and moved with uncon-scious grace toward him. "My lord?"

He cupped his fingers around her chin and lifted her face to his. "Five years, Sharah. Why do you still insist upon calling me 'my lord' when we're alone? I've asked you not to."

She cast her eyes downward. "You are King Darius, ruler of all Persia. I am your concubine."

He stifled his impatience. "You are my beloved."

"I am your property, taken from my people as you swept through my country in your quest to expand your empire."

"How could I have left you?" he whispered roughly. "One look at that beautiful face of yours and my heart was lost."

Her dark eyes flashed fire at him. "Yet you keep me prisoner."

"Prisoner, Sharah? Gaze around you. What do you see? This is not a prison. This is one of the finest rooms in the palace." In anger and frustration he jerked the miter from his head and hurled it across the room. "No, I am *your* prisoner."

Darius's temper was legendary, and his action would be guaranteed to send brave men scurrying for cover.

Sharah simply met his hard gaze with a soft question. "Then I'm free to leave?"

"You know I cannot allow that. I cannot live without you. I will not."

She smiled sadly and turned away.

He caught her by the shoulders before she could put distance between them and brought her back against his body. "Is my presence in your bed so displeasing to you?" he murmured, his mouth at her ear.

She closed her eyes as pleasure shivered through her. "You know it is not. You are a very skilled lover. My body responds to you even when my mind wills differently. But the blood of the Karzana that runs in my veins demands I must be free to go to my people when they need me."

"*I* need you. Give me your love, Sharah."

"Gladly. When you give me my freedom."

He sighed heavily, and gradually his hands loosened on her shoulders until they dropped to his side.

The heat between their bodies disturbed her.

She took several steps away before she faced him again.

He pulled a red bag from the folds of his *candy*. "I have brought you a present that I have had made especially for you." She did not respond. Darius smiled inwardly. His Sharah—so stubborn, so proud. "Hold out your hands," he said softly, and when she did, he pulled the silken strings loose and upended the contents into her hand. Out spilled a long rope of large, matched pearls. The clasp was a pearl that had grown in the shape of a heart.

Unable to stop the gasp of admiration that rose naturally to her lips, she lifted the necklace to the light. Each pearl was an object of perfect loveliness, creamy white in color, blushed with a soft pink.

Darius took them from her hands and carefully laid them around her neck. "These are my gift of love to you, Sharah," he said quietly.

She looked down at the pearls that fell over her breasts to reach to her knees, and within her proud soul another scar was carved. Darius had given her the extraordinary pearls to try to make her forget that even birds could fly free, but not she.

She raised her head, sending her hair rippling to her waist, a silken black cascade. "Am I free to do as I wish with these pearls?"

"Of course. They are yours."

She moved to one of the tall, arched tower windows. "Then I may throw them away?"

An expression of surprise crossed his face, but he nodded, wanting to humor her out of her sad mood. "Yes, although I wish you would not. It took a great deal of time and effort to collect pearls so perfectly matched."

"But may I throw them away?" she insisted.

Frowning, he said, "If you so desire."

She glanced out the window to the ground some hundreds of feet below. "And may I jump after them?"

"No!" Horrified, he raced across the room to pull her away from the window. "Sharah, what are you thinking of? If you jumped, you would be killed."

Gravely she stared up at him. "So I am free to do with the pearls what I will, but not myself."

"Sharah—"

"You gave me the pearls freely as a gift of your love. I, too, want to give you my love freely. But as long as I am kept against my will, I cannot."

"Sharah, how can I let you go?" His voice broke with his anguish. "You are my life."

She touched his face, so dear to her heart, and softly smiled. "No, Persia is your life. But you will have me, my dearest. Let me live as I was meant to be—free, like all those of my tribe, to shelter under the wide sky and ride with the winds. If you do this for me, I promise I will always come back to you."

"Sharah, I cannot . . ." He stopped as he saw her determined expression. "I have no choice, do

I? I must surrender you to the sky and the winds if I am to keep you at all."

She gathered his strong hand in both of hers and raised it to brush the palm with her lips. "You won't be sorry. I may not always be here when you want me, but I will always be here for you when you need me."

And so Darius had his goldsmith put on the gold backing of the pearl clasp a special mark. It was two intertwining circles, without beginning or end, and symbolized Darius's and Sharah's eternal love for each other.

And for the rest of Darius's life Sharah came and went from the palace at will. It was reported that at his death, Sharah, wearing her lover's pearls, was by his bedside. Then she and the pearls disappeared, never to be seen again at the court of the Persians. But the story of their love and the pearls was told far and wide until it grew into legend.

One

The old Gypsy woman deposited a long, gleaming rope of pearls into the hands of the dark-haired, dark-eyed young woman sitting across the small table. *"These pearls will bring you good luck. Soon a man with cinnamon-color hair will come into your life and magic will follow."*

Leah shivered, just as she always did when she heard one of Zarah's predictions. But she slowly shook her head. "You know I don't believe in magic."

"My child, you have been exposed to the mystic ways of the Gypsies since you were a small girl. You may not *think* you believe in magic, but deep down you know the truth—there are many things beyond the ordinary and that cannot be explained."

Since arguing with Zarah was fruitless, Leah simply smiled at the older woman, then bent her head to study the rope of pearls. Myriad candles illuminated the interior of Zarah's gold-colored tent, and in the subdued light the pearls gave off a breathtaking luminosity that seemed to spill onto Leah's hands, investing her skin with an almost unearthly radiance. Leah had a drawer full of beads and other trinkets that Zarah had given her over the years, but this necklace . . . "Are you sure you want to give this to me? It's so lovely."

"The pearls belong to no one and therefore are not mine to give. But I sense you are troubled. I want you to take the pearls, wear them."

She was troubled, but she was no longer amazed that Zarah could sense her moods. She had been five years old when she had wandered alone into the Gypsy camp and seen Zarah for the first time. The nineteen years since had not changed her opinion that Zarah was the most beautiful and the wisest woman she had ever known.

"You always seem to read my feelings," she murmured.

"What is it, my child?"

"The radio station where I work has been sold, and I'm worried about what the change will mean."

"But you are the station manager. Surely they won't make any changes without your consent."

Zarah had a beyond-the-normal understanding of many things, but business was not one of them, Leah reflected lovingly. "The organization that bought the station is known to be very tough," she explained. "They could fire me and bring in someone else. Or they could do away with the station altogether. We're very small, you know."

Zarah reached across the little table and ran an aged hand gently down Leah's sable-brown hair. "Oh, my child. In many ways you are as fragile as a butterfly, but you also have much strength you have yet to discover. Put the necklace on. Good things will happen to you, you will see." While Leah dutifully looped the necklace around her neck, Zarah eyed her with humor. "You haven't said anything about the cinnamon-haired man I predict you will meet."

"Zarah—"

The old Gypsy woman held up her hand. "Never mind. You have a Gypsy heart, good and true. Soon you will believe. But for now it is enough for you to know that I desire happiness for you as much as I desire it for Rafael, the son who was born of my body."

"I do know that." From outside came the sound of laughter and guitars, but Leah was reluctant to leave the tent. As a child, she had often taken naps on the daybed at the back of the tent as Zarah read palms and told fortunes. The tent had always been a place of safety and fascination to her, and the years had changed nothing. The rich fabrics seemed as worn as always, and the scarlet, gold, and green colors seemed as faded. The scent, too, was the same, flowery and vaguely mysterious. A cluck of Zarah's tongue brought her out of her reverie.

"How many other young women who had been

given such a necklace would wait this long to see how it looked on them?"

Leah grinned and got to her feet. "Sorry."

The cheval mirror in the corner cast back the expected image of a young woman who was slender and of average height, and who possessed large, velvety brown eyes and sable-brown hair that fell past her shoulders in soft, flowing, natural waves. She had worn the three-year-old skirt and blouse many times before—the blouse, a royal blue, off-the-shoulder peasant style; the skirt, full and tiered in colors of red, fuchsia, green, and royal blue. Leather sandals protected her bare feet.

But as familiar as the face, body, and clothes in the mirror were, there was also something different. Amazingly the pearls around her neck seemed to exude energy, and their lustrous beauty radiated outward to reflect onto her, making her skin luminous and . . .

"They make me look . . . almost beautiful."

Soft wonder tinted Leah's voice, and behind her, Zarah smiled. "Perhaps it is just that the necklace is making you see yourself as you were meant to be—shining and happy."

Leah went to the Gypsy woman, knelt down beside her, and laid her head in her lap. "I'm going to miss you so much, Zarah. Can't you stay a few more days?"

Zarah placed her hand gently on Leah's head like a loving benediction. "The stars have a time schedule all their own that we should not question. Haven't I taught you that? Now listen to me, my child. Tonight is the last night of the carnival. Tomorrow the men will start to prepare for our next journey. So go outside, have a good time, enjoy the night."

Leah stood and brushed her hand down her skirt. With her movement the unfamiliar weight of the pearls shifted across her breasts. "You're right. I'm taking up the time of paying customers. We can talk tomorrow."

Zarah caught Leah's wrist with a surprisingly strong grip. "You are more important to me than the money of the *gaje*. Never forget that."

To cover the fact that her eyes were misty with tears, she bent and pressed a kiss on Zarah's cheek. "I won't."

Outside the tent, Leah paused to blink against the sights of the carnival. Colored lights were strung in every available tree, around the booths, and on the rides.

Growing up, she had waited with impatience for early summer, when the Gypsies would come and stay for two glorious weeks. When she had turned eighteen, she had gone to live with the Gypsies, traveling with them for three years. The carnival crackled with color and vitality. She loved it and considered herself part of it.

But tonight the color dazzled, the lights seemed especially bright, and the sound struck her with a sense of unreality, because it was *too* real. She felt she had stepped out of Zarah's tent and into another dimension, and could not adjust to the warmth, gaiety, and energy of the night.

There was something different about this night, she realized, and she was a part of it.

Nothing seemed real. Not even she.

Everything seemed too real. Even she.

Could it really come from the magic of the pearls? Leah quickly answered her own question. Of course not; she didn't believe in magic.

She made her way through the carnival crowd, calling out greetings and stopping often to speak with one of the Gypsies. Slowly her cares drifted away. When she spotted Rafael, she headed toward him.

He was leaning back against a big elm tree, one hand holding a cigarette, one foot braced against the tree's trunk. He watched her approach from beneath permanently shadowed, heavy-lidded eyes. "Hello, pretty little girl," he said softly when she was near.

She grinned. He had said the same thing nineteen years before when he had found her wandering the camp, and over the years it had become his standard greeting to her. But no matter how often Rafael called her "pretty little girl," her mother had told her with more frequency that with her dark hair and eyes, she looked too much like the Gypsies to be pretty. As the years had gone by, she'd learned that it was really her father she favored—the father who had deserted her mother when Leah had been born, the father who had been killed in an airplane crash two years later. But knowing the cause of her mother's bitterness hadn't made her persecution any easier to bear.

Her mother had been dead for three years, but the power and the hurt of her words and actions remained with Leah.

"Taking a break?"

He nodded, brought the cigarette to his mouth, and drew heavily on it. "Mikalo is spelling me at the booth." Rafael was a skilled and gifted silversmith. During the winter months, when he and his tribe lived in Florida, he crafted exquisite jewelry and ornamental dishes.

"He won't have many customers," she said, singing her words with a teasing lilt, "because all the ladies will wait until you get back." Rafael was five years older than she and like a brother to her, but that didn't keep her from appreciating his darkly handsome looks.

His mouth twitched with amusement. "Don't start."

"Hey, it's not my fault women think you're sexy. It's that brooding, mysterious quality of yours—it creates all sorts of fantasies in the ladies' minds. I hear them talking."

"Leah—" He broke off, and his gaze lifted to a point behind her.

Curious, Leah glanced over her shoulder and saw Sheila Donaldson staring with meaningful intensity at Rafael. Sheila's blond fairy-tale beauty was emphasized by the pastel-flowered silk chiffon dress she wore, and the matching long, trailing scarf around her neck. Leah turned back, all teasing forgotten. "Rafael, you must be careful."

"The warning is not necessary."

"You don't understand. I live in this town, and I know things you don't. Sheila is married to a very prominent man. It's an unhappy marriage, and she's vulnerable."

He dropped his cigarette and ground it out with the toe of his boot. "I've heard all about her unhappy marriage and the husband who emotionally abuses her. You of all people should have a sympathy for her."

"And I do, but right now my concern is for you. Last summer . . . well, I noticed certain things between the two of you. I suspected you might be seeing her, but I thought—Rafael, don't do anything stupid."

He lightly flicked her cheek with a long brown finger. "Hey, you're not to worry about it. There won't be any trouble. My affair with Sheila ended last summer."

Leah's smile held relief and apology. "I'm sorry. It's none of my business. It's just that—"

"Where there is love, there is concern. I understand, and we can forget the matter." He touched one of the pearls at her neck. "I see Zarah gave you the necklace. She said she was going to."

She laughed. "These pearls look just like the real thing, don't they? Not that I've ever seen the real thing."

"What is real or not real is in the mind of the beholder. They are lovely and so are you." He paused. "Did Zarah tell you what she saw for you?"

"Magic." Her tone conveyed her opinion of magic.

"And your life has been filled with hurt, not magic, so you don't believe."

"Rafael, take the pity out of your voice. People live whole lives without believing in magic."

"Ah, but what kind of lives do they live?"

"Good lives, I'm sure. And," she added firmly, "my life is fine, thank you very much."

He gave a tug on her hair. "Not by Gypsy standards, and they are the only standards that matter."

Her brow furrowed with sudden curiosity. "Zarah has never told my future before. What are you two up to? Do you want me to go back on the road with you? Is that it?"

He smiled. "We've always wanted you with us, you know that. We stole you when you were six, didn't we? You would have been raised a Gypsy if that witch of a mother hadn't come to get you. But now Zarah has given you the pearls and . . ."

When he didn't continue, she prompted him. "Yes? And what?"

"And you have your job at the radio station."

"Is that really what you were going to say?"

He stared at her for a moment, his black eyes enigmatic, then he grinned. "No, I was really going to say that we *used* to want you on the road with us, but not anymore. When you were with us, you had this tedious habit of giving the customers the right amount of change. It ruined our reputation."

"You're one of the most honest men I know, Rafael. In fact, I'm probably the only thing you ever stole, so stop teasing me."

"But why, when pretty little girls are so much fun to tease?" He gave another yank on her hair. She lunged for him, but he was quick and ducked behind the tree. Laughing, she went after him.

Stephen Tanner docked his speedboat and started for the carnival. Restlessness had driven him from his house and onto the lake. He had skimmed over the water in his new, sleek, jet-engined boat, and for a while the speed had fed his need for action. But when he had seen the lights of the carnival, he had cut the engines, and for perhaps five minutes he had sat out on the lake watching the lights and listening to the music and the laughter. Then, in a spur-of-the-moment decision, he'd geared up the boat and wheeled toward shore.

He supposed he could chalk up his unexplained urge to investigate the carnival to the fact that he was having trouble relaxing in his new country home. The house had been completed only a few weeks before, and this was the first time he'd tried to stay the night.

The sight of the Gypsy woman standing beneath the tree, smiling up at the Gypsy man, interrupted his thoughts and brought him to a halt. He wasn't sure why she interested him. She wasn't doing anything extraordinary. Although she was quite lovely, she was no more lovely than any of a dozen women he knew.

He looked closer. Maybe it was just his restless

state, he thought, disturbed, but the colored lights behind her appeared alive, almost as if they were giving off a pulsing sensation. It seemed to him that she belonged with the lights, as if she were one with their vividness and their animation.

He squeezed his eyes shut, opened them again, and saw something different: a hauntingly still essence that intrigued and baffled him. How could she seem to be part of the pulsing vitality of the lights, and utterly tranquil at the same time? He had to be seeing things that weren't there.

Suddenly she moved, grabbing for the man, who feinted before taking off around the tree. Laughing, she went after him. They were playing like children, Stephen realized with surprise, and he wondered what it would be like to be able to abandon oneself to play. Or to anything besides work.

The thought passed, but his fascination for the Gypsy woman continued. When she slipped on a muddy patch of ground, his body tensed, instantly ready to help her, but the Gypsy man quickly grabbed her, preventing her from falling.

Amazed at his reaction to her, Stephen turned away, took a few steps, stopped, and turned back just in time to see the two embrace and each head in opposite directions—the man toward the carnival, the woman toward the pavilion.

Stephen followed her.

At the pavilion Leah kicked off her sandals, turned on the water spigot, knotted the hem of her skirt high up on her thigh, and stuck her muddy foot and calf into the cool stream of water.

Watching the mud melt away, she remembered how a few minutes in Zarah's tent had banished her heavy heart. It had always been that way. Except this time Zarah had given her the pearl necklace and a strange prediction. As if a necklace could make a difference . . . With one foot and calf clean, she stuck the other leg into the water.

"Hello."

Her head jerked up and her pulse lurched with alarm at the sight of the tall man standing in front of her. A man with *cinnamon*-color hair.

He'd been wrong, Stephen thought. She wasn't as lovely as any of a dozen women he knew. Her beauty was incomparable, and right now she was tensed with the hesitancy of a wild thing, trying to decide whether to bolt. He held out a hand. "Don't be afraid. I only want to talk to you."

Slowly she straightened and stared at his hair with large, wary eyes. The color *had* to be a coincidence. "Talk to me about what?"

"You speak English."

Her dark looks had led him to believe she was foreign, she realized. In fact, he probably thought she was a Gypsy. "I'm American."

"I'm sorry. I didn't mean to offend you."

"You didn't."

The town of Sunnyvale lit the pavilion with utilitarian fluorescent lights. The colored lights of the carnival were yards behind her, but the feeling remained with Leah that the reality of the night was too vivid, too loud, and therefore had blurred into an illusion of the mind. Was *he* an illusion?

His face was incredibly strong, and the cleft in his chin looked as if it had been put there with a hammer and chisel. Masculinity and sex appeal emanated from him in an amount almost guaranteed to unbraid a woman's equanimity. Under normal circumstances he was a man whom she would avoid, but the night seemed to be having a strange effect on her. Unsure about what to do, she unconsciously lifted her hand to the pearls. At their touch she felt her nerves of apprehension gradually dissolve. "What did you want to speak to me about?"

He shrugged as if what he was about to say were incomprehensible to him. "I saw you and followed you. I wanted to speak to you, but I'm not sure about what." He smiled.

She almost took a step backward. She imagined a charming shark would have a very similar smile.

"I guess you expect that," he murmured.

"Expect what?"

Her skin had a dark golden sheen to it, like honey in the sun. But there was no sun and he couldn't see the moon from where he stood. Still, the need to touch her was irresistible. He brushed his fingers along her bare shoulder. "Expect men to want to talk to you."

His touch was a revelation to Leah because of the warmth that surged then lingered on her skin; but emotional scar tissue protected, and the urge to run came naturally.

Somehow he sensed her intention and put his hand on her arm. "Don't."

She jerked away from him. "Do you usually command with just a word or a touch?"

His brows drew together. "Why would you say that?"

"Because you were so sure I would stay."

"You're wrong," he said gravely, aware that their conversation verged on the extraordinary. *She* verged on the extraordinary. "I wasn't sure at all."

Her emotions in turmoil, she bent to turn off the water, still tingling where his fingers had held her. When she straightened, she had unknotted her skirt and had her sandals dangling from her fingers by their straps. "Where are you from?"

"My business is headquartered in Dallas."

She made a motion with her head that sent her hair rippling over her shoulder. Now she understood. This man was a stranger who had no preconceived ideas about her. The notion was oddly stimulating. "I knew you weren't from around here."

"How?"

"Because I *am* from around here. I was born and raised in Sunnyvale."

He glanced toward the carnival, his confusion apparent. "But I thought you people traveled . . ."

"You people?"

"Gypsies."

"I'm not a Gypsy, although sometimes I feel like I am."

"But I saw you with the Gypsy man beneath the tree."

"That was Rafael, and he's a good friend."

"Really? That's interesting. I'd always heard that Gypsies never let non-Gypsies into their ranks."

"They don't." With a whirl of colored skirt and sable hair, she started back toward the carnival, her bare feet covering the uneven, sometimes rocky ground with ease.

"Wait a minute."

She heard him come after her and realized he was actually interested in her. All she had to do was let him catch her. *Magic,* Zarah had said, and Zarah had never told her anything that wasn't true. Maybe . . . just for tonight . . . it wouldn't hurt to believe. A heady excitement replaced her panic and made her feel strangely bold.

He caught up with her and fell into step beside her. "What's your name?"

"Leah," she said, glancing at him from the corner of her eyes. His body in motion was a study in measured power. In fact, everything about him was controlled. His chinos showed no wrinkles and fit over his hips and long legs with tailored perfection. His shirt was by a well-known designer and short-sleeved, but his arms, while appearing strong, showed no bulging muscles. Her instincts told her that he was deliberately restraining his strength and sex appeal and that she must be cautious.

But magic didn't always take instincts into account.

"I'm Stephen. Stephen Tanner."

At the spot where the illumination from the colored lights began, she stopped, looked up at him, and decided to be honest with him. "Did you know that you have cinnamon-color hair?"

He chuckled. "My mother calls it reddish-brown."

"I hope she doesn't say your eyes are just green."

"Why not?"

"Because green is not an accurate description. They're the color of a pine forest, cool, dark, and . . . they make me want to walk into them."

"What's your full name?" he asked softly.

"Leah Jayne Kellerman."

His glance dropped to her mouth, then returned to her eyes. "So, Leah Jayne Kellerman, where are we going?"

"We?"

"We," he said firmly, but with that charming smile she was sure could slice without warning into tender skin. "Letting you out of my sight would be impossible for me at this moment."

"Why?" She felt like a baby taking its first steps. The freedom was exhilarating, but she knew that a fall could be painful.

"Because you're fascinating, and you're beautiful, and I want to get to know you better."

She'd been fishing for a compliment, but in no way was she prepared for it.

He grinned. Her large brown eyes were very expressive, and her astonishment was genuine. When would she stop intriguing him, he wondered. "Besides," he added, "I've never been to a carnival before."

Her amazement was apparent. "You haven't? But that's awful."

He gestured toward the carnival. "Show me why."

She hesitated. Spending time with him would be risky; she wasn't used to taking risks. On the other hand, she was as familiar with the carnival as she was with her own heartbeat. Here she would be in command, her steps would be sure and on firm ground, there would be no danger of falling. And there was the necklace . . . and the night. She took his hand. "All right."

At the Shetland pony ride they watched while Toma, a teenager with black curly hair and infinite patience, coaxed a four-year-old boy out of his fear, then sat the child astride a pony. Toma looked up, saw her, and sent her a wink. She smiled, and with a toss of her head led Stephen on.

At the Ferris wheel, she asked, "Would you like to take a ride?"

"I don't think so." He gazed up at the top seat as it swayed, while at the bottom of the wheel, a couple was being let out. "Hanging in the sky in anything that doesn't have a jet engine doesn't appeal to me."

"I've ridden that wheel countless times, but I've never ridden in a plane before."

He looked at her oddly. "You've *never* ridden in a plane?"

"No. You see, it's unnatural to fly through the

sky with a casing of steel around you and artificial air piped in for you."

"Oh, the air isn't artificial. It's real, but it's just—"

"If you're going to fly, you should do it like the birds do it, free, unencumbered, and without someone else choosing your flight pattern."

"Flight pattern?"

"Besides, flying in planes is just too organized. Seats all in a row. Attendants in uniforms, serving everyone food with the same texture and design. You know, this Ferris wheel is perfectly safe. Kore is an excellent mechanic."

It took him a moment to catch up with her abrupt change of subject. "Kore?" He glanced at the elderly Gypsy man at whom she was smiling. "Do you know them all?"

"*Them?* They're not a species of insects. Gypsies are a proud, noble, and ancient race." Aware that her voice had risen sharply, she stopped and began again. "Yes, I know all of the Gypsies. Their carnival has been coming to this town for years."

He glanced around. "I didn't mean to be disparaging. It's just that I haven't noticed the Gypsies being friendly with any of the other townspeople."

"You won't."

He could count the minutes he'd known her, but he already realized she was the most complicated woman he'd ever met. He was convinced that if he smoothed his hands over her body, he'd actually be able to feel a network of finely tied-together nerves running beneath her skin.

She tossed her hair so that it fell behind her shoulders, and he caught a subtle, sensual scent of dark velvet flowers that made his imagination reel.

"Do you want to ride the Ferris wheel?" she asked once more.

"Maybe later."

She grinned. "You're making it very difficult for me to show you the carnival. You don't seem to want to do anything."

"That's because I'm not interested in the carnival. I'm interested in you."

Just then a man in his late twenties bumped into Leah's back. The man looked over his shoulder with a smile of apology, but the smile faded when he saw her. "Sorry," he said, and with a quick nod, walked away.

Stephen's gaze followed the man, a frown on his face. "Who was that?"

"Gary Mercer. He's a teacher at the high school."

She turned away, unwilling to explain about being raised by a mother who barely tolerated her. And how at a very early age, bewildered and lost, she had turned to the Gypsies for the love her mother couldn't give her. But the townspeople hadn't understood. They had seen a child who was allowed to run wild with the Gypsies, wearing colorful ragtag clothes Zarah made for her, and they had viewed her and her mother as strange and different. While accepting the entertainment the carnival provided as a break in their routine and appreciating the percentage of the take the

Gypsies paid to the town, the people had an inherent mistrust of the Gypsies and kept their distance. They kept their distance from her as well, and she had never gone out of her way to try to change their treatment. She accepted it just as she accepted that tomorrow the town would be buzzing about how she had been at the carnival with a stranger who wasn't a Gypsy, and about how she had actually been comfortable enough with him to hold his hand.

Her gaze suddenly dropped to their joined hands. His was a strong, capable hand, and she wondered what Zarah would make of his palm. "How would you like to have your fortune told? The woman who tells fortunes here, Madam Zarah, is very good."

"I don't believe in things like fortune-telling and astrology," he said firmly.

"No?"

He shook his head. "Do you?"

Rolling a pearl back and forth between her fingers, she gazed at his cinnamon-color hair. Like a drowning person reaching for a life preserver, she tried to grasp reality one more time before the night completely got away from her. His hair color had to be a coincidence, and her reaction to the night could be attributed to the fact that she was off balance because Zarah, Rafael, and the others would be leaving in a couple of days.

She told herself these things but in the end was unsure if she'd been successful in convincing herself.

"It's best not to discount something just because you don't understand it," she murmured.

He paused to wonder if she had answered his question, then concluded it didn't matter. The reflection from the colored lights blended their hues into her dark brown hair like shining ribbons. "What would you like to do?" he asked softly.

Something told her that he normally used that soft tone in only two situations: when he was seducing a woman and when he was threatening a man. But he hadn't been trying to seduce her. The softness had been meant to soothe, and so she decided to stay with him a while longer. "Let's just walk around."

"Leah," Bertole, a short man with a well-rounded body, shouted, as they passed his booth. "Bring the *gajo* over here."

"What's a *gajo*?" Stephen asked in a whisper.

She laughed. "That's you. A non-Gypsy. Come on." She pulled him over to the booth and explained the game. "One ticket will get you three balls. For every furred wooden cat you knock over, you win a prize. One cat gets you your choice of prizes on shelf one. Two cats gets you your choice of prizes on shelf two. The best prizes are on shelf three." She nodded toward the stuffed bears and dogs on the top shelf.

He gave Bertole two dollars, and the Gypsy set six balls in front of him. "I warn you, I never even played Little League."

"It's only a game," she said encouragingly. "What do you have to lose?"

"I'm not sure." He cast a dubious glance at Bertole, who smiled benignly back at him, then he turned to consider the prizes. "I think I'll win you that red teddy bear up there, Leah. Would you like that?"

Bertole rolled his eyes, his disdain plain. Leah thought of her enormous stuffed animal collection that the Gypsies had given her over the years. "You don't have to win me anything."

"But I want to."

In the next minute, six of the worst thrown balls Leah had ever seen sailed past the wooden cats without even ruffling their fur.

Bertole gave a hoot of derision. "Leah could knock down three cats in a row by the time she was eight."

Leah sent Bertole a dark look. "Stephen, let's try another game."

He slapped two more dollars down on the wooden counter. "I never give up."

Laughing, Bertole lay six more balls on the counter. The first two balls Stephen threw brushed the fur of two different cats. The third ball knocked down a cat. The rest of the balls missed altogether.

"Chose a prize from shelf one," Bertole said.

"Not on your life." Stephen produced another dollar. "I'm determined to win Leah that teddy bear."

"It seems I'm going to get very rich tonight," Bertole said cheerfully.

Stephen stared with concentration at the furred

cats, and Leah caught Bertole's eye and pulled at her ear. The Gypsy grinned and nodded.

Stephen suddenly cut his eyes to Bertole. "Don't you dare take them down for me."

Leah flushed guiltily, but a grudging hint of admiration edged into Bertole's eyes. Gypsies had no respect for people who were easily duped.

Stephen pointed a finger at her. "I don't need or want my ego stroked."

His sudden burst of anger directed at her took her by surprise and forcibly reminded her that he was a stranger whom she didn't know at all. Her chest tightened until it hurt for her to breathe. Her skin went clammy. She felt herself withdrawing, pulling in all the emotions she'd been so bravely exposing. It was a defense mechanism that stemmed from the times when her mother's diatribes against her would become particularly virulent and Leah's tender feelings could take no more. It was then that she'd search for the still peaceful place inside her to escape to.

But this time she was too angry with herself. She stayed and tried to face the situation. How could she have been so foolish as to let her guard down with this stranger? He would be driving back to Dallas tonight; tomorrow he wouldn't even remember her or this night. She didn't see Bertole's concerned look because her gaze was fixed on the back of Stephen's head.

He threw the first ball. A cat went down, as did two more cats with two more successive throws.

When he handed Leah the teddy bear, he was clearly satisfied with himself.

"Thank you," she whispered.

"You're welcome. Now what shall we do?"

She backed away from him, holding the teddy bear tightly to her chest, its softness acting as a buffer against the pain she felt trying to penetrate her. "I've shown you everything. You should leave now."

Completely bewildered by her reaction, he reached for her, but she flinched away. "What's wrong, Leah?"

It was beyond her to explain. "Nothing. You've just seen everything there is to see, that's all."

He closed the distance between them, this time taking care not to touch her. "I don't want to leave, Leah. I want to spend more time with you, and even if I have to get on that damned Ferris wheel, I will, if only you'll get that haunted look out of your eyes. Give me some help here. Are you angry with me for some reason?"

Her grip on the teddy bear tightened, pressing several of the pearls into her skin, and she remembered the necklace and Zarah's prediction. Little by little her confidence returned, and with it, reason. *If* he had been seriously angry with her—and she was no longer sure whether he had been or not—his anger certainly hadn't lasted, and it would seem he hadn't been rejecting her. He wanted to be with her to the point of being willing to do something he didn't want to do. Maybe if she kept reminding herself that tonight was special, illusory, and magical, everything would be all right.

She pointed to the ride closest to them. "How about the tilt-a-whirl?"

Stephen nodded his head. Damned if he knew what had just happened. For a minute there, Leah had looked at him with all the fear and vulnerability of a wild creature in great danger. What was going on?

"Maybe this whole carnival is enchanted," he said, "and you're a witch who has cast a spell over me. At this point the explanation makes as much sense as anything. Let's go."

She settled into the seat beside him, but kept her eyes averted. Rico, another teenage Gypsy boy, brought the bar down that would hold them in. She handed him the teddy bear and her sandals. "Will you put these somewhere for me? I'll get them later."

"Sure thing, Leah." Rico threw Stephen a suspicious glance, then went on to the next group of people.

"Could I put my arm around you?" Stephen asked.

"You're supposed to hold on to the bar."

"Leah, it's going to be very hard not to touch you on this ride."

"You're right, I suppose."

"Does that mean I can?"

He was amused and stymied. He'd known women who had been willing to hop into bed with him after a two-minute acquaintanceship, and Leah had to think about whether she'd let him put his arm around her.

"That means yes," she said.

The tilt-a-whirl began moving, and the car swiveled wildly while the whole ride turned and lifted.

Leah's torso slammed against Stephen's and centrifugal force kept their bodies fast to each other. The lights around them blurred together until Leah could see only colored streamers. The individual notes of music and squeals of laughter melded. A long, unmeasurable length of time passed. . . .

The ride slowly came to a stop. The world stilled. Colors and sound separated once more into their distinct identities.

Neither Leah nor Stephen moved.

"I have a boat at the dock," he whispered. "Let's go for a ride out on the lake."

The carnival was familiar territory to her. She had been taking baby steps there, but out on the lake . . . Her hand went to the necklace, and the feel of the pearls lent her courage.

Two

The boat skimmed over the midnight-black lake with Stephen at the wheel and Leah beside him. The speed, the night, and the man made her feel as though her blood had turned effervescent and was sparkling and bubbling through her veins. The wind whipped her laughter back to her, surprising her with the sound of her own joy.

She was feeling a freedom that she usually felt only with the Gypsies, a release from the constraints that normally bound her. Her baby steps were growing into giant steps, and she didn't want to hear the small voice in her brain that cautioned it was impossible to walk on water.

When they reached the middle of the lake, he cut the motor, and she pushed a handful of wind-blown hair from her eyes and looked questioningly at him.

"I thought it would be nice just to drift awhile."
He held his hand out. "Come sit with me."

He was going to kiss her, she realized suddenly.
The idea excited and frightened. She was twenty-
four years old and had never been kissed passion-
ately by a man before. What would it be like, she
wondered. Would she be disappointed? Would he?
Her heart was pounding so hard, she didn't hear
him say, "Leah?" until he repeated himself.

She looked at him, startled. "What?"

His smile was gentle, and he brushed an errant
wave from her face that she had missed. "Why do I
get the impression that you're about to dive into
the lake and swim back to shore?"

The breeze was cool, and wavelets lapped hyp-
notically against the boat's hull. In the distance
the lights of the carnival were soft, and the music
floating across the water was faint. "I guess because I was about to."

His expression was one of absolute fascination.
"I don't think I've ever had that effect on a woman
before. I'm not sure whether I should be flattered
or insulted."

She bent her head, looking at nothing in particular. "It's not your fault. It's just that sometimes,
I'm . . . shy. No, that's not right. Sometimes I'm . . .
afraid." The necklace, whose length hung below
her waist, caught her eyes with its iridescent glow.
As she picked up one of the pearls, his chuckle
sent a warmth skittering through her.

"I promise you I'll do nothing to make you want
to jump overboard. In fact, if you'll look at me and

smile, I'll even start the boat up and take you back to shore."

Slowly she raised her head, meeting his gaze, but she didn't smile. "Don't do that. I'd like to stay out here for a while. The breeze is cooler here, and it's quieter."

"Quieter?"

"Except for two weeks out of the year when the Gypsies bring the carnival to town, I lead a very quiet life."

"When I first saw you, there were colored lights behind you. They were pulsing. It seemed to me that you belonged with the lights. Then I noticed the stillness in you and decided I had been wrong."

"You were right both times," she said simply.

"You know," he said after a moment, "there was a time tonight when I wondered at what point you would cease to fascinate me. Now I know that such a point doesn't exist. Let's go sit at the back, and you can tell me all about the colored lights and the stillness in your life."

Her smile came slowly, and its loveliness made his knees weak. "I'm not sure I want to, because if I did, you'd be the one jumping overboard."

"Try me." He led her down the center aisle of the big boat to the stern, where he chose a wide-cushioned, sofalike lounge and brought her down beside him.

The moonlight rayed across the lake and high-lighted the compelling strength of his face. Who was he, she wondered, and why had he come to the carnival? A moment's thought brought her to the decision that it might be better not to question. After all, he was a stranger who would disappear at the end of the night. But before the night ended . . . "First, I'd like to ask a favor of you."

"What's that?" A sudden brief rush of wind lifted the ruffle of her peasant blouse and caused it to flutter about her throat. Without thinking, he smoothed it back into place and, in doing so, brushed his hand over her breast. The momentary contact was enough to make him go hard with need. Her next words left him aching.

"Would you kiss me?"

"That's the favor?"

She nodded.

Most women he knew initiated what they wanted. Most women offered no surprises. But then, he was quickly learning that Leah wasn't "most women." She constantly enchanted and astonished. "Why would you *ask* something like that?"

"Because the waiting is awful."

She had a way of addressing his questions from an angle that before tonight he hadn't known existed, and it was like being hit between the eyes with a stunning freshness.

"You certainly know how to get to a man," he said in a voice made husky by growing desire. Stroking a finger across her bottom lip, he felt her lip tremble. "Oh, yes, you certainly do." He lowered his head and lightly touched her lips with his. "There's no need to tremble," he whispered. "At least not yet." And then he moved his mouth back and forth in a sure, unhurried way that grazed the soft flesh with gentleness until he felt the trembling stop and her mouth grow silkily pliant.

He brought his hand to her neck so that it cradled her jaw and controlled the angle of her head, then he hardened the kiss by degrees until her lips parted and his tongue could delve into the depths that awaited.

Leah felt as though the universe had expanded. She'd never known such feelings existed. Fire that made her shiver, sweetness that made her melt. Without hesitation she reached for his shoulders, then wound her arms around his neck, wanting more, needing more.

How had he lived this long without kissing her, he wondered, deeply stirred. He'd never known a kiss like it. He felt caught in the middle of a kaleidoscope with changing patterns all around him that were made up of colors, light, and Leah. And each new pattern made him want her more, until he reached the point where he didn't think he'd be able to stand not taking her.

He pulled away, suffering physical pain as he tried to draw air into lungs that felt as if they'd never breathe again. "We'll go to my place."

"That was my first kiss," she whispered.

The shock he had felt at the fire of their kisses was nothing compared to what he felt now. "I don't believe it. You were incendiary."

"It was my first."

"But you seem so"—he searched for a word—

"worldly." The minute he said it, he knew he was wrong. She was *other*worldly.

All her defenses went up. "Just because I've never allowed a man to kiss me doesn't mean I'm not worldly. My mother never permitted me to date while I lived with her. When I was eighteen, I left home and went to live with the Gypsies. They were very protective of me when it came to men."

"Gypsies? Protective?"

She wasn't surprised at his conception of Gypsies, but nevertheless it made her sad. "It's not necessary to be worldly-wise to be experienced. My experience was gained by learning to survive— here in Sunnyvale and then when I traveled with the carnival. Sometimes I think I've had too much experience at surviving, because sometimes I think I'm too good." Her eyes held sadness and wisdom beyond her years as she looked at him. "Then other times I don't think I'm good enough."

He shook his head, feeling the need to clear it. "I don't understand."

"It doesn't matter," she said quietly.

"The hell it doesn't."

"Stephen, it doesn't matter. We met only two hours ago."

She had just said something logical, and he pounced on it. "*Exactly.* So why tonight for your first kiss? Why me?"

She shrugged. "It just seemed right."

"Right?" His voice rose and filled with incredulity. "Honey, if it had been any more right, we would have both gone up in flames."

Suddenly she laughed, at herself, at him, at their situation. "You're right. We kissed great."

He stared at her a long moment. "I'm not going to be able to figure you out, am I?"

"Why would you want to?"

"Oh, I don't know. How about to preserve my sanity?"

She grinned. "I'm not sure I know any sane people."

"Everyone I know is sane."

"Then we have nothing in common."

His hand closed around her throat, above the pearls. "We have the fire in common."

Her grin faded. "Yes, the fire. Perhaps we should leave well enough alone."

His thumb began to massage up and down the cord of her neck. "Can we?"

"Of course." The passion of the kiss rushed back full force to her, and she was vaguely aware that she put no trust in what she had just said.

"For someone so inexperienced, you're a very good liar," he said, and kissed her softly.

The care with which he kissed her made her feel scorched right down to her fingernails. "Lies are sometimes necessary for survival," she said when she could breathe again.

"So are kisses."

"Where do you live?"

He straightened away from her and rubbed at his brow. "Do you do it deliberately?"

She moistened her lips to ease the parting of his lips from hers. "What?"

"Do and say things that throw me. Never mind. I live right . . ." The boat had drifted, and he twisted around, sighted in the shore to get his bearings, then pointed. "There. Do you want to go over?"

Her gaze followed his finger to the newly built, modern, two-story cedar and stone house that sprawled on the shore. "So that's *your* house. Everyone was wondering who the owner was. You used Dallas contractors and labor, you know."

"Ah, yes. I was told they were the best."

"There were people around here who would have been equally as good and could have used the work. There was some resentment about the matter, and the Dallas people stayed to themselves, so no one gave anyone a chance to work out the problem."

"How do you know all of this?"

She shrugged. "It's a small town." The lake breeze was not cooling her heated flesh. She stood, took a few steps, then turned. "It's a nice house."

"Thank you," he said, amused. Somehow after all the money he had spent on the house, he'd rather expected something more than *nice*. "I built it because my friends, one of whom is my doctor, told me that having a country home would help me learn to relax and rest."

"And has it?"

"The first night's been a washout as far as relaxing goes." The way he looked at her made his meaning clear.

Her cheeks warmed. "I'm sure you'll get the

knack of it soon." She studied the house. "You left on several lights."

"I always do."

"That's something else we differ on. I never leave lights on. In fact, I prefer stars to lights."

"Most people don't have stars in their homes, so they have to settle for lights," he said, watching her. Her face was in profile to him. Sable-brown waves caressed her cheek and a moon-thrown shadow contoured her jawline. She was staring toward the shoreline, idly playing with the pearl necklace.

"There are times I can find peace only when I'm beneath the sky." It was something the Gypsies had taught her. Although they all had trailers, they spent as much time as possible beneath the velvet night sky.

"Do you often have trouble finding peace?"

She turned grave eyes on him. "Yes, but tonight there's been a different kind of peace that hasn't really been a peace at all, yet it's been every bit as nice. I really think it's the magic . . . and you."

He surged to his feet and took hold of her arms. "Let's go to my house and turn off the lights."

She knew that if they went to his house, they would make love. The heat between them was simply too strong for them not to make love. But in a few hours this night would be over, and when she woke up in the morning, she would be just plain Leah Jayne Kellerman again, Leah Jayne Kellerman accepted and loved only by the Gypsies.

"I think it's time I went back to the carnival."

"Stay, Leah. Stay with me."

She gazed solemnly into his eyes. "Tomorrow will be better if I don't."

A look of absolute frustration came over his face. "I can't even imagine what you mean by that."

She put her hand on his shoulder in a comforting fashion and wished she could comfort herself. "It's all right. It really is." Behind him she could see the lights from the carnival begin to go out. "Kiss me one more time before we leave."

He pulled her hard against him so that she could feel every line and bulge of his body. "If I kiss you, I won't stop, and that one kiss will last for the rest of the night. Is that what you want?"

"Yes . . . but I can't have it."

"Yes, you can. It would be the easiest thing you've ever done. All you'd have to do is say kiss me, Stephen."

She wanted to swallow, but she couldn't. Neither could she pull away from him. Her breasts were full and aching and crushed against his chest. Her lower body was throbbing.

"Kiss me, Stephen," she whispered. His hands tightened on her arms, his head began to lower, and she added in a louder voice, "But let me stop the kiss when I need to."

"Dammit, Leah."

He brought his mouth down on hers.

And the fiery contact almost split the night apart.

•　•　•

Stretched out under the sky in her backyard for the rest of the night, Leah longed for peace and sleep. They never came. When morning broke over the horizon, she found that the tomorrow she had said would be better if she didn't make love with Stephen was not better at all.

Tomorrow without Stephen hurt.

Lying on the quilt, gazing up at the gradually brightening sky, she remembered how hard it had been for her to end their kiss. And when she had, it had been as if something vital near her heart had been torn.

But as soon as she'd pushed against him, he had released her, started the boat, and taken her back to shore. Before he had handed her onto the landing, he had taken her in his arms and given her another kiss, this one soft and gentle. Then he had said, "I'm letting you go for now, but I'm not letting you get away from me."

She *had* gotten away from him, though, and it was for the best, she told herself. Firmly shoving him from her mind, she rose and went into the house to plan her day while getting ready for work. With any luck she could leave the radio station early and have that much more time with Zarah.

In her bedroom she tried to draw from the secure, warm environment she had created for herself. Ivory lace curtains fluttered at the open window. Cheerful rose striped wallpaper covered the walls. A wicker chaise lounge boasted plump velvet pillows that carried a small floral design. A fluffy sky-blue cotton comforter lay across the old wooden bed she had painted with white enamel. A rose and blue flannel quilt draped a round table that held a hammered silver mirror Rafael had made for her, along with a fringed lamp and an assortment of small pictures of her Gypsy friends. A pot of white tulips sat beside the bed. A straw hat that featured a band of red and pink cabbage roses decorated a corner.

She chose a white cotton two-piece dress to put on. Before heading out the door of her bedroom, she paused. The pearls lay on her dresser in lustrous splendor, the morning sun highlighting their soft pink blush. Zarah would be expecting to see them on her, she reflected. For Zarah she should wear them.

Deciding to use the necklace as a belt, she wound the pearls around her slim waist three times, then secured it by tucking both ends back into the pearls.

After a moment's hesitation she raised her eyes to the mirror. The pearls gleamed radiantly against the white cotton. As she had last night, she saw and felt their energy. And they made her look, well, very nice, she thought, immediately casting aside the superlative description that had been on the tip of her tongue. But her step was a bit lighter as she left her house.

Leah had been living and traveling with the Gypsies three years when her mother had died.

She came home with the idea of selling the house and returning to the Gypsies. But after she'd been in Sunnyvale a few weeks, she'd come to the startling realization that she didn't *have* to leave again. And there was also the feeling that she had relied on her friends, the Gypsies, long enough. Perhaps, she had thought, it was time for her to create a life within which she could function as a productive and independent individual.

And so, just as leaving home at the age of eighteen had been a step for her, so, too, was returning to stay.

Almost simultaneously with the drawing of these conclusions, she read in the paper that there was a position open at the local radio station, KSUN, for an assistant to the station manager. The more she thought about the idea, the better she liked it. She knew that KSUN programming was inconsistent and boring and that the community interest in the station was negligible. The challenge intrigued her. She got the job, learned the business, and succeeded to her boss's job when he resigned.

The station had come to mean a lot to her. Everything that was broadcast from six in the morning to nine in the evening had her stamp on it now. She supposed it was her way of reaching out and touching people without risk.

The radio station was housed in a rectangular brown cement building. There was nothing Leah had been able to do about the drab color on the outside. The owners had refused to sink any fresh money into the operation of the station, and they certainly hadn't been concerned with aesthetics. But with as much of her own money as she could spare, she had seen to it that splashes of color were everywhere on the inside of the building, from the blue of the curtains to the pink, green, and turquoise patterned slipcover she had sewn for the couch. Bright, vivid posters covered her office walls, and healthy green plants grew along the windowsill.

"Good morning, Leah," Margaret, the receptionist, said as Leah entered the building. "I have a message for you from a Mr. Roland, who called an hour and a half ago. He said to tell you he'll be driving from Dallas and should make the trip in about two hours, depending on the traffic in Dallas. Who is he anyway?"

Leah made a face. "He's TCIC's accountant."

At the mention of the new owners of the station, Margaret went pale. She was a widow in her late fifties who, because of her age, had had trouble finding employment. When she came to interview for the receptionist job at KSUN, Leah had seen the potential for a dependable, levelheaded, and loyal employee and had hired her on the spot. She had never regretted her decision. Now she tried to alleviate the older woman's distress.

"He only wants to look at the books. Everything's in order." Or will be, she thought, as soon as she had an opportunity to bring the books up-to-date. She usually did the bookkeeping in the evenings, but when Zarah, Rafael, and the Gypsies were in town, she spent that time with them. If she'd just had a chance to talk with this man before he'd started . . .

"I know he won't find anything out of line, Leah. I'm just worried that TCIC will feel our profit margin isn't great enough for them to keep us. If I lose this job . . ."

Margaret's anxiety tugged at Leah's heart. She understood what it was like to not be able to fit in anywhere or to be accepted. For her, Margaret, and most of the others who worked at the station, KSUN was a haven where they could function in a useful, hassle-free way and create something that was their very own.

She gave a brief smile to Margaret. "Try not to worry. I'm going to do my best to see that none of us loses our jobs." And if she only knew how she was going to do such a thing, she thought, then she could stop worrying too.

She bypassed her office and made her way down the hall. At the large broadcast-booth window she waved at Harry Morrison, who acknowledged her with a nod. "Everything okay?" she mouthed.

He nodded again.

A smile lingered on her face as she walked back down the hall to her office. Harry was a Vietnam veteran whose memories of that war had left him unable to hold down a full-time job until Leah had hired him. He didn't talk much and was happiest when he was in the control booth, surrounded by albums and tapes, and playing the mixed fare of pop hits and classic rock that he loved so much.

She took a seat behind her desk and wondered

how Pat Meredith, her advertising salesperson, was doing. Two days earlier, Leah had talked with Pat about a plan to bring in a substantial number of new accounts. She hoped to show TCIC officials that increased profit was a realistic possibility so that they wouldn't be quick to make changes. The plan meant double the amount of work Pat usually did, but she had quickly agreed. Pat was dedicated to Leah and the station because Leah and the job had given her acceptance at a time when she was desperate.

Pat was a twenty-one-year-old young woman who, two years earlier, had had a darling little boy named Bobby out of wedlock. The father had been a boy she had met at college. As soon as he had heard Pat was pregnant, he had left her high and dry. Pat's parents had disowned her. With no means of support and no one to care for Bobby while she worked, she had jumped at the chance to sell advertising for KSUN. For the first year of Bobby's life he had been carried papoose-style on his mother's back while she went from merchant to merchant selling advertising spots on the radio. And even though she was now making enough money to hire someone to care for Bobby, Pat still carried him with her a great deal of the time.

Leah sighed and stared down at the memo pad she had been doodling on. How had the name *Stephen* gotten there?

"You look very beautiful this morning," he said from the doorway.

She jumped. "How did you get in? How did you find me?"

He strolled casually into the office, stopping only when he came up against the front of her desk. "That's three questions, but I think I can handle them. A very nice lady out in the lobby directed me to your office is the answer to your first question."

"She usually notifies me of any visitors."

"I convinced her not to." His smile was the one that mixed charm with predatory sharpness. "Finding out where you worked was equally easy. As you said last night, this is a small town. And if you'll recall the last thing I said to you, you'll have the answer to your third question."

"You said you weren't letting me get away from you," she said slowly, "but I did get away. At least for a little while."

He bent over the desk so that their faces were level. "No, you didn't. You weren't free of me a minute. I was with you all night. Just like you were with me."

"That's not true."

"Really?" He straightened. "Tell me something. Where did you sleep?"

"Outside."

He nodded with satisfaction. "No peace, Leah. Just like I had no peace." With a quickness that did nothing for her emotional balance, he rounded the desk and hauled her out of the chair. "Do you know why we had no peace? Because we needed like hell to be together."

The kiss came as no surprise to her. Neither did the fact that desire flamed up in her so quickly she was left weak. Last night she'd experimented with his kisses and become an addict. He was right, she reflected hopelessly. Need for him was twisted all through her, a painful part of her that she felt each time she drew a breath.

He'd spent the night recalling her kisses, Stephen thought hazily, yet memory hadn't come close to the reality. He'd never known a woman with such instant, uncensored responses. It excited him as nothing ever had. The nerves that ran just beneath her skin were charged with currents of fire and emotion. And every time he came near her, kissed her, or touched her, she pulsed just like the colored lights. He was determined she would pulse for no one but him.

He slid his hand to the soft fullness of her breast.

"Stephen," she whispered on a sigh.

"Tell me you couldn't get away from me last night." He pressed kisses over her face while thumbing at the nipple through the cloth of her dress. "Tell me I was crawling through your bloodstream, just like you were through mine."

She gave a little cry. "Yes, oh, yes."

With a hard shudder he drew away and stared down at her with eyes as dark as a forest at night. "Okay, then, what are we going to do about it?"

"I—"

"You didn't need me to teach you how to kiss last night, Leah. You won't need me to teach you how to make love. After we come together, there may be nothing left but ashes. I think it's more than worth the risk. What do you think?"

She wasn't sure she *was* thinking, and she didn't care. "I agree," she whispered.

He yanked her back to him and kissed her fiercely.

At first she didn't hear the intercom.

"Tell her you're taking the rest of the day off," he muttered against her lips.

Her brain was filled with clouds and fire. "What?"

He raised his head. "Your receptionist is calling you on the intercom. Tell her we're leaving."

The clouds in her head parted. The fire remained. She turned in his arms and punched the intercom button. "Yes, Margaret?"

"That man is here," Margaret whispered.

Leah closed her eyes. Only one person would cause Margaret to lose her composure—the accountant from TCIC. "Give me five minutes, then bring him in." She released the button and looked up at Stephen. "I'm sorry, but I've got to see this man. It's important."

"I thought what we were planning was important."

"It is. I—I just have to see him."

"Then I'll wait."

"No." She pushed against him, but he didn't release her. "Stephen, you've got to leave. I'm going to be nervous enough without you being in the room."

He raised one reddish-brown brow. "Nervous? Then all the more reason for me to stay, I think." He stopped her next objection with a deep, thorough kiss. When he was done, he said, "I'll be sitting right over there in that corner, and when you're through, we'll go to my house." He kissed her again, more lightly this time. "Okay?"

She smiled her surrender. "I guess I don't have any choice, do I?"

"No." With an answering smile he retreated to the corner of her office and sat down.

Leah quickly straightened her dress and ran a hand through her hair. As she brought her hand down, she brushed the pearls at her waist. The contact with the necklace reminded her of Zarah's prediction. She had said a man with cinnamon-color hair would come into her life and magic would follow. By anyone's standards, that part of the prediction had certainly come true, Leah decided.

At first she hadn't believed in the magic. Then she'd chosen to think that the magic would disappear with the night. But irrefutable proof that she'd been wrong now sat in a corner of her office. And she had to admit that since she'd been wearing the pearls, she had felt and acted differently. Her appearance had even changed for the better.

The other part of the prediction had been that the pearls would bring her good luck. She was certainly going to need all the luck she could get if she was to save the station, she thought, unaware that she was running her fingers back and forth across the surface of the pearls.

The door opened, and Margaret ushered in a tall, slim man with a face that Leah decided looked rather like a ferret. She tried to remember. Weren't ferrets used to hunt down small animals?

"Miss Kellerman, I'm Mr. Roland with TCIC."

"Yes, I know. I've been expecting you. Won't you sit down?"

"Yes, thank you."

He took the chair she indicated, and Leah eyed him warily, having already forgotten Stephen. "I was notified by registered mail of the sale of KSUN some time ago, but you're the first person from that organization who's contacted me. What can I do for you?"

He folded his hands across his chest and stared hard at her. "I'd like to see your books, naturally."

Doing her best not to be intimidated, she graciously nodded her head. "Naturally." This was where the sticky part came in. "It's just that I wish I'd been here when you called. I could have saved you a trip today."

His head came up as if he had gotten a delightful sniff of something not quite right. "Oh, and why is that?"

"Because I need to make several entries before the books will be up-to-date."

"Why do *you* need to make these entries? Don't you have a bookkeeper?"

She gritted her teeth, not sure why she was letting this irritating man get to her. She'd certainly had to deal with more objectional people. "This is a very small station, Mr. Roland, and as I'm sure you can appreciate, I watch our expenditures very carefully to make sure that we show a profit. By my doing the books, I save an additional salary." And I can pay better salaries to Pat, Harry,

Margaret, and the others, she silently added to herself.

"Whether or not you are qualified to do the books is something I will, of course, look into. In the meantime, when will the books be ready for me to see?"

She did some quick calculations in her head. The men would be tearing the carnival down today. That meant the Gypsies would be leaving tomorrow or, at the latest, the next day. And then there was Stephen. "A week," she said quickly. "Maybe ten days."

"I'm afraid that's unacceptable."

She'd been told all her life in one way or the other that what she did was unacceptable. Sometimes it hurt; other times it made her angry. This time it made her angry, and she didn't bother to hide it. "And I'm afraid, Mr. Roland, that that's the best you're going to get."

He sat forward and jabbed a finger at her. "My dear young woman, you can't possibly understand who I am."

"I am not your dear young woman," she snapped, then could have bitten her tongue. She had to try to keep her feelings under control.

"*Who* and *what* you are may very well change after I see those books. TCIC has sent me here—"

"*That's enough,*" Stephen said suddenly, causing both Leah and the accountant to jump in surprise.

The accountant turned around, saw Stephen, and sprang quickly up. "Mr. Tanner, I had no idea you were here—"

"And I had no idea that anyone representing my company used such high-handed tactics." He came to his feet in a leisurely motion.

Leah was the only one in the room still seated. "In *your* company?" she said, stunned. She felt as if she had two separate pieces of information that belonged together but she couldn't quite make them hook together.

"I think it's time you left, Roland," Stephen said, his eyes on Leah's pale face. "I'll see you back in Dallas."

The accountant glanced between the two of them. "But—"

"Good-bye, Roland." As soon as the man was out of the office, he asked, "Are you all right, Leah?"

"Your name wasn't on that registered letter I got, was it?" she asked slowly.

"No. One of my executives sent the notification."

"And the TCIC. What does that stand for?"

He sighed and rubbed at his brow. "Leah, I can see where you're going with this, but there's really no reason—"

"*What* does the TCIC stand for, Stephen?"

"Tanner Communications and Investment Corporation."

She nodded. She was no longer stunned, nor was she confused. Anger and strength were growing in her by the second. "And just *when* were you going to tell me it was your company that had bought the radio station where I work?"

He slipped his hands in the pockets of his slacks

and eyed her steadily. "I don't know when it would have occurred to me. I had other, more important things on my mind."

"Of course you did. The same thing that's been on your mind right from the first—seducing the little Gypsy girl with the mud on her feet."

He brought his hands down on her desk and leaned close. "That's not the truth and you know it. You may be angry, Leah, but keep the game fair."

With an abrupt motion she pushed away from the desk and jerkily stood up. "Game, Stephen? Is that what this is to you?"

He closed his eyes for a moment and lightly massaged them with a finger and thumb. "Game was the wrong choice of word. I'm sorry. But the fact of whether or not I own this damn station has nothing to do with us. I just found out this morning that you worked here. If I hadn't, I wouldn't even have come here."

"You own it, and you wouldn't even have come to see it? Now I understand how you could employ someone who looks like a ferret."

He almost questioned her use of ferret, but he caught himself in time. "Let me try to explain this, Leah. Under my direction, TCIC recently took over Banner Industries. When we did, we automatically acquired all of Banner's holdings. KSUN wasn't my interest in the company, and it was a *very* small part of the acquisition." He made a gesture toward her. "Do you understand?"

"You may think I'm strange, but I hope you don't think I'm stupid."

His fist came down on the desk. "Dammit, Leah, stop twisting what I'm saying. Understand that I'm very probably falling in love with you. And understand that KSUN's profits for the year wouldn't buy a day's supply of paper clips for TCIC. And understand that those two facts have nothing in the world to do with each other."

His words hit her body with a different kind of force and impact. Her mind allowed her to absorb everything but his belief that he was very probably falling in love with her. To her it wasn't a fact, but an impossibility.

She'd found love and acceptance only with the Gypsies, and even a blind man could see that Stephen Tanner was as different from the Gypsies as night was from day. He had reached out and taken a handful of the world and it had not rejected him. In fact, the world embraced such men as Stephen Tanner, whereas it rejected people like her, Zarah, and Rafael.

For a little while she had thought magic might be possible. But now she understood that he wanted her only because she was different. His fascination for her wouldn't last.

"Leah, did you hear me?"

"You're going to sell KSUN, aren't you?"

Stephen felt like tearing something apart, piece by piece. He drove hard fingers through his hair. "For God's sake, Leah? *What* is going on inside you?"

"Aren't you?"

He sighed. "Probably. The station is not important in TCIC's overall business."

"It's almost the whole world to me and the people who work here."

He'd never seen anyone look so vulnerable and at the same time so well-guarded. He could deal with someone vulnerable, and he could deal with someone well-guarded, but how in the hell did he deal with both at the same time? "We'll work it out," he said quietly.

She wrapped her arms around herself. "Not between you and me, we won't. We are just too different. We have nothing in common."

"We have the fire."

She stared at him, emotion-laden silence and space separating them.

When the office door burst open, it was all Leah could do to wrench her gaze from his. Then she saw the anxious face of the nine-year-old Gypsy boy. "What's wrong, Bandi?"

"Zarah sent me to get you, Leah. Rafael is in jail."

"*Jail?* My God, what happened?"

"The *gaji* woman, Sheila Donaldson, was found dead this morning, and they're saying that Rafael murdered her."

Three

Leah's first sight of Rafael behind bars nearly stopped her heart. He was sitting on a bare-mattressed cot, his back against the wall, his arm resting on his raised knee, a cigarette in his hand. Enclosed in the small cell, locked away from the sun and the wind, his spirit had already begun to shrivel; she could sense it without him saying a word.

"Let me in," she said to Tim McCafferty, the young deputy sheriff who had guided her back to the cell area.

" 'Fraid I can't do that, Leah. Rules. He's been arrested for murder. That means he's considered dangerous and not allowed any visitors except for a lawyer, which he's refused."

Leah turned her head and looked at Tim. "Rafael won't hurt me and you know it. Now, do you want to search me for weapons?"

Tim's gaze dropped from hers. "Uh, no. I know you wouldn't bring in anything you shouldn't."

Leah's grin was involuntary. "No, you don't. You just don't want me to tell Pat that you searched me." Tim and KSUN's advertising salesperson had become quite an item as of late.

"Aw, Leah—"

"Are you going to unlock the door, or do you want to give me the key and let me do it?"

"I'll do it." Tim placed the key in the large lock, turned it, then slid open the heavy door. "I can give you only ten minutes."

"Alone, I hope."

He nodded.

She entered the cell. When she heard the door clang shut behind her, she knew immediately how Rafael must feel. She had the sensation of walls closing in on her and air being sucked from her lungs. Steeling herself against succumbing to panic, she sat down on the cot so that she faced Rafael. When he didn't say anything, she touched his hand. "Rafael? How are you?"

He took a hard pull on his cigarette. "Great."

"I don't understand why they think you killed Sheila, but they've made an awful mistake."

"They didn't make a mistake," he said tonelessly. "In fact, they followed procedure perfectly. Late last night, then again early this morning, they received an anonymous call. The first call told them they would find her body at her husband's fishing cabin, the second call said I had been there last night and told them the two of us had had an affair. They searched my trailer and found the rings and gold necklace she had been wearing. They couldn't do anything else but arrest me."

"But you *didn't* kill her."

The corners of his mouth lifted slightly. "No, I didn't." Reaching out, he gently caressed her cheek. "Pretty little girl," he added softly. Then he leaned his head back against the wall and closed his eyes.

"Rafael, talk to me. Tell me something that will help me get you out of here. You said someone placed you at the cabin last night. Were you there?"

"Yes. Sheila had asked me to meet her there, but I was late . . . too late." He fell silent.

"Rafael?"

"It will be all right," he whispered without opening his eyes. "Go now."

Deeply troubled, she went to the cell door and called for Tim.

Sheriff Johnson was a big, robust man with whom few dared to argue. Although Leah knew him by sight, she had never had occasion to talk with him. The fact that Rafael was in jail pushed all these considerations aside. "Rafael didn't kill Sheila," she said as soon as she entered his office.

He looked up from the form he was filling out. "Evidence says otherwise."

"Can't you see a frame when it stares you in the face?"

He leaned back in his big leather chair and

propped his booted feet on the desk. "So you think he was framed, do you?"

"I know he was. It's obvious."

"If it's so obvious, then tell me who you think framed him. Tell me who you think killed Sheila."

She thought fast. "Her husband. It had to be."

"Husbands are always the most likely suspects. Can't you do better than that?"

"But everyone knew they had a bad marriage."

"Bad marriages can be fixed real easy with divorce, Leah."

Frustrated, she clenched her hands at her side. "Didn't you even question Robert Donaldson?"

He grinned. "Don't you think after all these years I know my job? Of course we questioned him, and Robert has an ironclad alibi. He was at his office in his appliance store, doing his books, just like he does every Wednesday night. The security guard saw him."

"Well, then someone else murdered Sheila, because Rafael didn't."

He sat forward, folded his hands on the top of his desk, and fixed her with a hard, level gaze. "Look, Leah. Maybe you're right. Maybe your friend didn't do it. But all the evidence points to him, and until I find out for sure that someone else murdered Sheila Donaldson, I'm keeping him in jail." He held up a firm hand when she prepared to argue. "As soon as it gets out that Sheila's been killed and that Rafael is a suspect, you know what's going to happen. Jail is the safest place for him."

He was right, she thought angrily. Dammit, he

was right. Tears sprang to her eyes. "But he can't breathe in there."

"I'm sorry, honey, he's got to stay." He paused. "But I'll tell you what I'll do. The law says I've got to charge a suspect or release him within seventy-two hours. I've already told you why I can't release him, and there's no doubt in my mind, at any rate, that I'm going to charge him. But I'll stretch the law and hold off officially charging him for a while, not long, mind you, but I can give you a few extra days to prove that he didn't kill her. Don't ask me to do any more than that."

The first thing she saw when she stepped outside the jail was Stephen, leaning against the hood of his car, waiting for her.

"I told you not to wait," she said, striking out along the sidewalk.

He caught her arm and gently guided her into the plush interior of his Mercedes. "And I told you that I would."

"Stephen, this isn't that big a town. Everyone walks."

He shut the passenger door, and she was left to impatiently finger the pearls at her waist while he walked around the car and got in. He inserted the key into the ignition but didn't turn it. "We need to talk, Leah. Do you want to go to your house or mine?"

"I don't have time to do either. I've got to get Rafael out of jail."

"You can't," he said flatly. "He killed a woman, and he's going to have to pay." Incredibly she laughed, but her laughter held a weariness and a sadness that ripped at his insides and made him fervently wish he could take his words back.

"I thought I might have to explain to you what it's like to be a Gypsy, but now I see I don't. You already know the world is hostile and suspicious toward them. And you already know they're outcasts. And the reason you know is that you're one of those people who have made them outcasts."

"Leah, I'm sorry I upset you. I know he's your friend—"

"Yes, he is. But even if he weren't, I would help him, because I understand what it's like to be an outsider. And, just so you'll know, you didn't upset me. In fact, I would have been surprised if you had reacted any other way." It was true that she would have been surprised, but it was a lie that he hadn't upset her.

"Listen to me, Leah. I've admitted right from the first that I don't always understand you, but that doesn't mean I don't want to. You say you feel as if you're an outsider. Tell me why."

For a split second she had the urge to go into his arms, rest her head against his chest, and pour out her pain and fears to him. Instead, she reached for the door handle. "I have to help Rafael."

His hand covered hers before she could open the door. "That's what the police are for."

"Sheriff Johnson is going to come up for reelection this fall. One more term, and he'll be eligible to retire with a nice fat pension. Do you really think he's going to jeopardize that and go against public opinion to help an outsider?" She shook her head. "No. Until I can prove to him that someone else killed Sheila and give him the name of that person, he'll keep Rafael right where he is. I'm Rafael's only hope."

"Then I'm going to help you."

"*You?*"

He rested his left forearm on the steering wheel and leaned toward her. "Leah," he said quite gently, "I run a multimillion-dollar corporation. I'm really very competent."

"A multimillion-dollar corporation is entirely different from a small East Texas town. Sunnyvale has got nothing to do with profit or loss. It's people. And, I think, sitting day in and day out in your big office in Dallas, buying and selling companies that you never even see, you've lost touch with people."

He eyed her consideringly. "Tell me, Leah, do you touch people?"

"What?"

"I have the feeling that you don't *touch* a lot of people yourself."

"Okay." She acknowledged his point and waited for the uneasiness she was sure would come at his perception. None came. "But I know the people of this town. I've watched, and I've learned a lot from life. I know—"

"So teach me what you know. I want to be able to see the world through your eyes."

"It won't work."

"Let me tell you something about myself, Leah. Up until last night everything I've ever done has had reason and logic behind it. But last night happened. I didn't see a lot of reason and logic then, and I haven't since. And I'm still here. I told you that I never give up. I also told you that I'm falling in love with you."

"You said *probably*."

"Did I say probably? I was wrong. I'm *definitely* falling in love with you."

The hammering of her heart was almost louder than the softness of his voice. "You're not falling in love with me. No one but the Gypsies has ever loved me. You'll eventually grow tired or angry or impatient with me, maybe all three, and then you'll go away."

He smiled, suppressing his longing to pull her to him and kiss her until she believed him. "If I go away, Leah, I'll take you with me. But in the meantime, if you want to try to talk me out of loving you, go right ahead. It may be the quickest way for me to learn what I want to know about you."

"I'm right, you know."

"No, you're not." He placed his hand on the key, ready to turn it. "Where are we going? My house or yours?"

She blinked. "Neither. I want to go see Robert Donaldson."

"Donaldson? The husband? Okay, then that's where we'll go." He turned the key, and the big car's motor purred to life. "Tell me how to get there."

Robert Donaldson was a handsome man, Leah thought, trying to be as objective as possible as she watched him pour himself a drink with slow, uncertain movements.

His holding up the crystal decanter of whiskey to her and Stephen was an afterthought of a man obviously numbed by the shock of his wife's violent death. "I'm sorry. Would either of you like a drink?"

"No, thank you," Stephen said.

Leah shook her head.

Robert replaced the decanter on the leather and walnut bar, started to sit down, then changed his mind. "I'm sorry," he said again. "You have to understand, this has been such a shock. I'm having a hard time dealing with Sheila's brutal murder."

"We understand," Leah said softly, "and I apologize for our intrusion, but I'd just like to ask you if you can think of any reason why she might have been killed."

He took a sip of the whiskey. "I know you're a friend of the Gypsies, Leah, but what I don't understand is why you're here. You probably knew about Rafael and Sheila before I did. The police told me this morning that my wife and your friend had been having an affair since last summer. That was the first I knew of it. Seems just about everybody knew but me." His fingers tightened around the glass until they were white.

Leah felt a sinking sensation in the pit of her stomach because there was no doubt in her mind that he was telling the truth. "I doubt very seriously if anyone knew, Robert, and besides, Rafael told me that their affair had ended last summer."

"Really? If that's the truth, and I'm not sure that I believe it is, then maybe that's why the filthy bastard killed her. Maybe he wanted it to continue."

Beside him, Stephen felt Leah stiffen. He reached over and covered her hand with his, hoping the physical contact would help.

"Rafael didn't kill Sheila," she said firmly.

"Then who did?"

"I don't know, but I'm going to find out. And that's why I'm asking you, can you think of anyone who might have had reason to want Sheila dead?"

As he gazed down at the dark amber liquid, the conflicting emotions that ranged over his face signaled that he was fighting for control. When he raised his head, it was clear he had lost the battle, and he turned his anger loose on Leah. "When I found out this morning that Sheila and that damned Gypsy had been having an affair and that they'd been meeting in *my* cabin, my stomach turned six ways to Sunday. So you listen to me, young lady. No one else in town had any reason to do it other than your friend, who, for my money, is exactly where he should be. Frankly, I hope they fry him."

Stephen stood and pulled Leah to her feet. "Thank you for your time, Mr. Donaldson."

He quickly helped her out of the house. As soon as they got into the car he asked, "What do you think?"

"I'm disappointed," she said frankly. "It's as clear as crystal that Robert Donaldson's in shock over his wife's murder. He's also angry because he's just found out about the affair. But he's not grieving. Not really. Given the fact that he and Sheila had a bad marriage, he's reacting exactly as I would have expected."

"That's what I thought too." He paused. "It was unpleasant for you. I hated seeing you go through it."

Surprise came and went in her eyes. "I'm used to it. I grew up in this town."

"That sort of thing may happen quite often, but you're not used to it in any way, shape, or form." He reached out and ran his fingers down her arm. "Your skin is too sensitive; there are too many nerves beneath it."

She looked at him oddly. "It was nice of you to be there with me."

His fingers tightened on her arm. "When will you get it through your head? What I'm doing is not nice. It's compulsory."

She was left without words. It was daylight. There were no colored lights. She was worried about Rafael. Yet Stephen was getting to her, pricking away at her lonely soul. She wasn't sure how to act, and just for a moment she panicked. Then her hand sought out the pearls. Something about them made her feel better.

He smiled at her. "Where would you like me to take you now?"

"I'm not sure," she said, pondering his question. "I guess it would be best if I go home. I've got to decide how to proceed and what I should do next. I've never done anything like this."

His fingers glided with a velvet touch up and down her arm, trying to lessen the intensity of her distress. "I have an idea. We missed lunch. It's nearly time for dinner. Let's go to my place. I'll make us something to eat, and we can put our heads together over the problem."

"Eat?" She hadn't realized until he mentioned dinner how hungry she was.

"Yes, you know, food."

"And you're going to cook?"

"I, uh, am going to try my best to serve you, my guest, something that will be edible."

She grinned. "That might be interesting."

"Then you think it's a good idea?"

"Actually I think it's a great idea."

He started the car, inwardly marveling. One minute Leah would be quiet, withdrawn into herself. The next, she would be the Gypsy girl beneath the tree, backed by the colored lights, laughing and carefree. She was a mercurial delight who baffled and entranced him.

• • •

Stephen watched as Leah gazed around the living room of his lake house and wondered at the cause of the wariness he saw in her eyes. "The architect followed my instructions to the letter," he said. "I wanted big open rooms with lots of windows. I figured if I was going to live in the country on a lake, I wanted a view from every room in the house."

She nodded but made no comment. Her eyes were on the magnificent linen drapes that covered the front wall of the room. The pattern of the fabric was in shades of blue and turquoise.

"Here, let me open the curtains," he said, matching his actions to his words, eager for her to like his house, "and you can see the great view of the lake. It gives the feeling of being outside."

"But we're not outside."

"No," he agreed. "That's true."

She nodded her head and turned her attention to the pale blue sofa. It had been custom made to curve around the large room in such a way as to form ingenious conversation areas. All along it, pillows in the same pattern as the drapes had been thrown to create artful comfort. Beautiful blue and turquoise silk cloths covered the side tables.

"My interior designer wanted to pick up the colors of the lake," he said, eyeing her intently.

"The lake isn't blue."

"But one always *thinks* of lakes as blue," he pointed out with determination.

She nodded. "Is the kitchen close by?"

Feeling defeat near at hand, he exhaled and gestured. "Past the staircase and right down that hallway. I'll show you."

The kitchen was bright and filled with the late afternoon sun. An array of copper pots hung suspended over a long wooden table of a highly polished bleached cedar. The cabinets were also made of bleached cedar. "My interior designer assured me that the countertop is the latest high-tech material. It won't burn, scratch, dent, or break, and it blends well with the cabinets." He looked at her expectantly.

She nodded, her eyes still holding the same wary expression. "Maybe we could cook outside. Do you have a grill?"

"A grill?"

"We could go to my house. I have a grill."

"I have a grill, Leah. What's wrong?"

"Nothing. Oh, look at the beautiful deck."

Before he could reach for her, she was out the back door. He caught up with her at the railing.

She drew in a deep breath as if she'd been starved for fresh air. "You didn't mention that you have a pine woods at the edge of your backyard."

He slanted his body so he could rest his arm on the top of the railing and see her face. "Now, why did I fail to tell you that, Leah? Why does there always seem to be something else to talk about?"

Hearing the humor in his voice, she looked into his eyes, whose color exactly matched the pines. "You have beautiful eyes, Stephen."

"Yours aren't so bad either." He wrapped a thick

strand of glossy sable hair around his hand, then released it. "What can I do to make you more comfortable?"

"I don't know what you mean," she said, her tone cautious.

"Uh-uh. I'm not going to let you get away with that this time. You're uncomfortable in my house, and I want to know why."

Her hands tightened on the railing and she gazed down at them. "You've spent a lot of money on this place."

"Forget the money."

"And the decorator must have . . . worked very hard."

"And you can forget the decorator too. Come on, Leah. Out with it."

"Well, it's just that everything"—she swallowed hard—"matches."

He wasn't sure he had heard her correctly. "Matches?"

She glanced quickly at him, then looked back down at her hands. "You know. Everything fits too perfectly."

"And that's bad?"

She took a deep breath. "Many people like it that way, but I never have."

Because *she'd* never fit or blended, he thought with sudden insight. He took her hand. "Come with me."

"Where are we going?" she asked, surprised.

He didn't answer but led her back through the kitchen, down the hallway, and into the living room. Once there, he dropped her hand and marched with purpose to the bank of windows. Because he had already opened the drapes, they were grouped at either end of the wall. He took a firm grip on the linen material and pulled.

"Stephen, what on earth are you doing?"

"Getting rid of these curtains. They're ugly." Half of the drapes fell to the floor to form a big mound of blue and turquoise.

"They're not ugly," she protested. "They just—"

"Match," he said, now at the other end of the glass wall. In moments the remainder of the drapes lay on the floor, and he turned his attention to the rest of the room. "The table covers, right? They're really awful."

"Stephen—"

Four table covers joined the drapes on the floor. He studied his handiwork, then took half the sofa pillows and threw them on top of the two mounds. "That looks better. The sofa will have to stay for now, but I think as soon as possible I'll get . . ." He trailed off and turned to her. "What would you do with this room?"

She hesitated. "I like arrangements that feature different styles, textures, and patterns. Nothing organized."

"That's just what I was thinking."

Suddenly she started laughing. "I can't believe what you've just done. Your interior decorator is going to have a fit."

"What interior decorator? As of ten minutes ago I don't have one."

Still laughing, she shook her head. "Are you aware that you did something that doesn't make sense?"

"Well, then maybe, for the sake of my mental well-being, I'd better do something that makes sense before I go into withdrawal."

"What?" she asked, suddenly breathless at the heat in the depths of his cool green eyes.

He went to her, and drew her to him. "Kiss you," he said. "It makes all the sense in the world to me. What about you?"

"No," she said softly.

His gaze dropped to her mouth. "Why not?"

"Because I want you to kiss me too badly, and it doesn't make sense."

"It's all right. All you have to do is say, kiss me, Stephen. And then hold on."

Her gaze locked with his. "Kiss me, Stephen."

Kissing him was like entering a brand-new world. Lights, colors, and feelings were strange and bright. It made her want to open up, to absorb his strength and his heat into her. He was so utterly male, he surrounded her, and she abandoned herself to the sensations of the kiss.

"For God's sake, don't do that," he muttered, his lips still against her mouth.

"What?"

"Respond like that." He cradled her face, his hands firm but with the slightest of tremors, and looked down at her. "You're not ready to go where a response like that could lead. But I most definitely am."

"You're talking about making love," she whispered.

"Ashes, baby. That's what may be left. Are you ready? Because let me tell you something, I sure as hell am. And if you keep responding to me like that, your choice may be taken away from you."

Her throat moved convulsively. "I want you to know something."

He moved the fingers of one hand caressingly over her cheek. "I'm listening."

"I want you, Stephen. I don't want you to be in any doubt. I've never felt this way before. You look at me sometimes, and it feels like those green eyes of yours have removed my skin and left only need. And when you touch me—"

His thumb came up and covered her lips. "Stop it," he said, his voice low, hoarse, and raw. "You're going to have to stop it, because I'm not going to be able to take the *but* coming after."

"But—"

His chuckle was a mixture of hurt and longing, plus a cutting kind of humor directed at himself. "See? This just isn't going to work, not right now, at any rate."

"I'm sorry."

"No," he said emphatically. "You've got nothing to be sorry about. You're wonderful. In fact, you're magic."

"It's not me," she said, "it's the pearl necklace I'm wearing."

He looked at her for a moment. "And I thought I was the only one who had anything to learn." He pressed a short kiss to her lips. "Let's go find my grill, then search my freezer for something appropriate to cook on it."

Out on the deck Leah watched the sun setting by infinitesimal degrees over the roof of Stephen's house. He was in the kitchen, cleaning up after their dinner, but he had the window open so that she could hear the stereo, which she had tuned to KSUN. Borodin's symphonic poem "In the Steppes of Central Asia" was playing, and she closed her eyes and let the music take her away to the windswept land about which Borodin had written so stirringly.

During the day Randolph Moore taught music at the high school, and this time every night he took command of the broadcast booth and chose from records that ranged from classical to easy listening. He had his own criteria for what he played, and she never interfered. People didn't particularly like him because he was sternly intellectual, but they enjoyed his choice of music, and homes all over town tuned in to his show.

The music ended, and "Somewhere in Time," the sound track from the movie of the same title, began. The beautiful, haunting melody fit with the peace of the pine woods, the lake, and the time of day, she decided.

When she opened her eyes and saw Stephen sitting across from her, watching her, she was surprised. "I didn't hear you come back out."

"That's all right. I didn't want to disturb you. You seemed caught up with the music."

"Music has always moved me."

"What else moves you?" he asked, curious.

"Pine woods." She tossed her head, letting the evening breeze play through her hair. Then she smiled as she remembered. "When I was a little girl, Rafael used to take me along with him on his walks through the woods around here. Sometimes I'd get tired, and we'd stop. We'd lie down on a bed of pine needles and stare up through the boughs at the sky and listen to the gentle whisper of the wind." Her smile slowly disappeared. "I wish he were here. He'd love the peace and beauty."

"I'm glad you like it."

"I'm going to get him out of there, Stephen. I have to. He'll die if I don't. He needs to be free to travel winding back roads that lead to places he knows and places he's never been. He needs to lie beneath a wide night sky."

"From what little I've come to know of you, he sounds a lot like you."

"Zarah says I have a Gypsy heart. I think maybe she's right. There's really only one thing I know for sure: I have to find out who murdered Sheila so that I can get Rafael out of jail. And I'm going to start first thing in the morning." A sudden look of guilt crossed her face. "I won't be able to be at the station full-time. And the books—"

He uttered an oath. "Don't worry about the station. I'm sure your people are competent. As for the books, you can burn them for all I care."

"But Mr. Roland—"

"Is back in Dallas, and KSUN's books are the last thing on his mind, believe me."

"When are you going back to Dallas?"

"I don't know."

"Before last night, when were you going back?"

He slowly shook his head and grinned. "You constantly surprise me. You used a straight line to get from A to B on that one, didn't you?" She smiled, and he shrugged. "Before last night I would have probably returned to Dallas today. Now I may never leave."

"You'll leave."

"I'm not going to argue with you about it. But one of these days, years from now, you'll look around and notice that I'm still here. And then maybe you'll accept the fact that you were wrong."

She fell silent, and not until the stars began to appear in the sky above them did she whisper what she was thinking. "You can't be right. But if you are, it has to be because of the pearls. What other explanation could there be?"

Four

Leah swung her feet over the edge of the bed, surveyed the floor of her bedroom, and let out a groan. The clothing she had worn the day before was scattered about. And the pearl necklace lay in one corner, gleaming with beauty and mystery.

The previous day's events, following her sleepless night after meeting Stephen, had taken their toll on her. Once Stephen had dropped her off at her house last night, she'd barely managed to undress before she collapsed onto the bed and fell sound asleep.

She slid off the bed, and as she went around the room picking up her clothes and the necklace, she thought of Stephen. Could it be possible that he would stay as he said he would? Could she really believe that in time he wouldn't reject and shun her, as most people did, because she was different and odd? More important, if she gave him her heart, would her heart remain safe?

Or was it too late to be asking any of these questions?

In the shower she pondered what her next investigatory move should be and quickly decided that she had to go see Rafael again. And this time he had to talk to her, because until he did, she had nothing to go on. She also wanted to see Zarah.

She dried off and donned a bright red sundress with tiny straps. In marked contrast to yesterday morning, there was no uncertainty about whether or not she would wear the necklace.

She scooped the pearls into her hands and stared down at them with wonder, no longer in doubt that they were genuine. Nothing fake could produce the mystique and the magic that this necklace did. Each pearl had been made, layer by lustrous layer, by a living creature deep in the dark depths of the ocean. And she was utterly amazed that for whatever reason, the necklace was in her possession.

Grasping the two ends of the pearl rope, she raised her hands. Midway to her neck with the necklace she froze. The string that attached the heart-shaped clasp to the necklace was frayed, leaving the clasp connected only by a few fragile threads.

Bands of iron began to contract around her chest. She felt as if she might suffocate. Oh, Lord, she must have somehow jerked the clasp last night when she had unwound the necklace from around her waist.

And now she couldn't wear the necklace until it was fixed.

She had to take the necklace to the jeweler. Immediately.

She quickly glanced at the clock. It was eight o'clock in the morning, and Mr. Ogilvy didn't open his shop until ten.

What was she going to do?

Calm down, she ordered herself. In her hands the pearls seemed to shimmer with strength and beauty; she clutched them tighter. Everything was going to be all right. Really. A wait of two hours wasn't going to make that much difference.

With a great force of will she relaxed her fingers and placed the pearls on the bed. Taking a step back, she wiped her damp palms down the sides of her skirt.

She jumped at the knock on the front door.

Stop acting foolish, Leah.

She made her way through the house to open the door.

"Good morning," Stephen said through the screen.

"Good morning."

"I like the blue color of your house. I couldn't really see it last night in the dark."

"It was gray all the while I was growing up. I hate gray. I painted it after I came back to town." She tried to draw a breath, couldn't, and turned to hurry back to the pearls.

He let himself in and followed. He found her in a back bedroom that was decorated with different textures, patterns, and colors, just as she had described last night. He liked it, he decided, then turned his attention to her. "Leah, what's wrong?"

"Nothing really," she said, digging in a bottom dresser drawer. "The clasp on the necklace is in danger of coming off, and I have to take it to the jeweler, that's all. What are you doing here?"

"I told you last night I'd be here first thing this morning to help you try to find out something that will help clear Rafael of killing Sheila."

She briefly glanced at him. "I thought you believed Rafael did it."

"Yes, well, I had forgotten about the law in America that says a man is innocent until he is proven guilty. You made me remember."

"He *is* innocent," she said, and tossed a bright blue scarf over her shoulder. Half of the contents of the drawer now lay on the floor.

"Leah, what are you looking for? Can I help?"

"I just found it." She held out a gold and red shawl to show him, then stood up and crossed to the bed.

He watched her carefully wrap the pearls in the shawl. "Have you mapped out a plan for today?"

"I'm going to go over to the jewelry shop. Then after the necklace is repaired, I plan to see Rafael again. Somehow I've got to get him to talk to me." She straightened, holding the red-and-gold-wrapped bundle to her chest.

"Maybe I could see him with you and—"

"Rafael wouldn't talk at all if you were there."

"Then I'll wait for you outside as I did yesterday. And there's no point in arguing," he added as he saw the expression of unease cross her face.

She fingered a piece of the fringe on the shawl. "I won't argue. It's just that I'm not used to having someone by my side when I have to face difficult things."

"Get used to it. I may not be able to help much in getting Rafael out of jail, because, as you say, I don't know this town. But at least I can give you moral support, and, in doing so, we can be together."

She tilted her head to one side and gazed up at him through dark lashes. "I don't know if I want to be with you."

He smiled. "Don't you, Leah?"

She did want to be with him, she thought. She just wasn't sure if she should or not. How could she trust a love that was being built on the strength of the magic exuded by a pearl necklace?

Leah peered into the window of Ogilvy's Jewelry Shop and spied Horace Ogilvy at the back. Horace was another citizen of Sunnyvale with whom she had never had much direct contact, but she knew him by reputation as a crotchety old man with a soft heart. She tapped on the window until she got his attention, then waved and gestured.

Horace Ogilvy squinted toward the window through his rimless glasses and saw her. His face settled back into its perpetual frown as he plodded down the aisle between the display cases to unbolt the door. "What is it, Leah? You know that I'm not open for business yet, don't you?"

"But it's five minutes until ten, Mr. Ogilvy. Can't you please help me out even though I'm five minutes early?"

He gave Stephen a suspicious glance. "Who's this?"

"This is Stephen Tanner. He's just built a new home on the eastern shore of the lake."

Mr. Ogilvy nodded his head. "You mean the house that was built by those Dallas people."

"That's right," she said. "Listen, I really need your help with my pearl necklace. The clasp is hanging by threads."

"Pearl necklace, you say?" He hesitated, but a glance at Leah's distraught face seemed to sway him. "Well, I guess I could give it a look. Come on in."

Once seated behind his workbench, he held out his hands. She unfolded the scarf and carefully laid the pearls before him.

His gray brows shot up. "I don't believe I've ever seen anything quite like this. It's remarkable. Yours, you say?"

She didn't know how to answer his question. Zarah had told her the necklace wasn't hers to give, but that Leah was to take the necklace and wear it. Did that mean that one day she would have to give up the necklace? The idea filled her with cold fear.

Mr. Ogilvy interpreted her silence in his own way, and his glance at Stephen proclaimed his conclusion. "Hmmph." He adjusted his glasses and turned to examine the gold backing of the clasp. "Strange mark. Interlocking circles. What does it mean?"

"I don't know," she admitted. "The mark was put there before I received the necklace."

"Hmmph. Well, I can fix this clasp for you, all right. No problem. Just have to reattach it to the necklace. Should be ready by tomorrow."

"Oh, no!" Panic rushed back to grip her. "I have to have it today. Right now, as a matter of fact."

He lowered his chin and stared at her over his glasses. "Right now?"

"Can we wait? Please? You said it wouldn't take long."

"I do have a few other things to repair, young lady."

"Please. Please?"

Stephen spoke for the first time. "If you'll do it now for her, I'll pay you triple what you would charge her if she picked it up tomorrow."

"Figures from someone who hired Dallas people," the old man muttered under his breath. "Leah, you can wait, and I'll have it for you in a few minutes. At my regular charge."

"Thank you, Mr. Ogilvy." She didn't even try to keep the relief from her voice.

"Hmmph." He bent his head to his task.

Stephen's lips twisted with amusement. "It's a good thing that I've already admitted that I don't know this town," he whispered, "because Mr. Ogilvy made your point in spades."

She took his hand without even realizing she was doing so. "It's all right. I don't know Dallas. Probably never will."

"You will if I have anything to do with it. Why don't we look around? We might find something you like."

He'd just made two disturbing suggestions: one, that they had a future together, and, two, that he would buy her an expensive gift. But she didn't have time to dwell on either of those disturbing remarks because he pulled her along with him to gaze into the display cases.

Graduation and birthstone rings filled one case. Charms, another. Diamond wedding ring sets, plus plain bands for both men and women crowded a third case. And the fourth case held men's rings.

"Too bad about Sheila," Mr. Ogilvy said casually, still working on the necklace.

Leah looked back at him, startled. "Yes, it was."

"Hard to believe. It's a real tragedy. She was in here just the other day too. Real happy, she was." He scowled absently and reached for another jeweler's tool. "Seemed most interested in one of those."

"Those?"

He pointed with the tool. "One of those men's signet rings."

She didn't need the pressure of Stephen's hand to prompt her. "Do you remember which ring she was looking at?"

"Of course I do." His words were almost growled.

"Do you think I'm senile? She was looking at that ring down there in the right-hand corner. The one with the M on it. Your necklace is ready. That'll be ten dollars."

Leah stared at the jeweler, riveted by what he had just said. *M?*

When she didn't move, Stephen went to pay him and gather up the pearl necklace in her shawl. "Thank you very much, Mr. Ogilvy."

"Hmmph. No trouble. And next time you build something out here, young man, you might consider using local workers."

"I'll do that."

"And, Leah? That young woman with the little boy that works over at the radio station . . . ?"

"Pat."

He nodded curtly. "Have her come by. I'm thinking of running a little sale. If the rates are right, I may advertise with KSUN."

"Thanks, Mr. Ogilvy."

Out in the car, Leah turned to Stephen, barely able to control her excitement. *"M.* We've got to find out whose name begins with M."

"Don't get your hopes too high. This may be nothing at all."

"No. It's something. I know it is." She touched his arm. "Listen, her husband's name is Robert Donaldson—no M there—and at any rate, she wouldn't be buying him a gift. Her father's dead. She has no brothers. Rafael's name begins with an R."

"What's his last name?"

"They go by their given names, Stephen. Anonymity is very important to the Gypsies. Most of them go through life without being registered anywhere. There are no birth or school records, draft or census—"

"What about a driver's license?"

She shook her head. "If they bother to get licenses, they usually register under false names."

He made a sound of disbelief.

"Intense secretiveness is the way they survive, Stephen," she said defensively. "When everyone is against you, it's best to have as few records as possible on yourself. And I'll tell you something else, if I don't know Rafael's last name, no other *gajo* does."

"Not even a woman with whom he went to bed and to whom he whispered words of love?"

"No," she said flatly.

"You're very loyal," he said, reaching out to brush a finger down the soft skin of her jaw. "Okay, then, you wanted to visit with Rafael. While you're doing that, I'll see if the sheriff managed to get a last name from him."

Leah's sensitive heart perceived changes in Rafael that would be barely perceptible to anyone else. The shadows beneath his eyes seemed darker, his brown skin paler, his lean, muscular frame thinner. And he was sitting in exactly the same position and place as he had been yesterday, as if when they put him in the cell, he had ceased to move . . . and to live.

Play the Loveswept Match Game

AND GET AS MANY AS SEVEN FREE GIFTS

THERE'S NO COST! NO OBLIGATION! AND NO PURCHASE NECESSARY!

HOW TO PLAY:

1. Carefully scratch off the three boxes at the right and match one, two, or three hearts with the hearts already revealed. You are eligible to receive one or more free books, and possibly other gifts, depending on how many hearts you match.

2. When you return the postage-paid card, we'll send you the books and gifts you qualify for — absolutely free.

3. A month later, we'll send you 6 new Loveswept novels to preview. You always get 15 days to preview them, before you decide. If you decide to keep them, each book is yours for only $2.09 — a savings of 41¢ per book (plus postage and handling).

4. You'll always receive your Loveswept books before they are available in stores. You'll be the first to thrill to these exciting new stories.

FREE—LIGHTED MAKEUP CASE

You may qualify to receive this tortoise-shell makeup case—if you match three hearts.

HOW MANY HEARTS CAN YOU MATCH?

Scratch off the three silver boxes with a coin! The more hearts you match—the more you get!

YES! I have scratched off the silver boxes. Please send me all the gifts for which I qualify. I am under no obligation to purchase any books, as explained on the opposite page.　　10355

NAME_____

ADDRESS_____APT_____

CITY_____

STATE_____ZIP_____

　　　　　　　　　　　　　　　　　　　　　1R1 2 3

1 HEART MATCH—
WORTH 1 FREE BOOK

2 HEARTS MATCH—
WORTH 4 FREE BOOKS

3 HEARTS MATCH—
WORTH 6 FREE BOOKS
PLUS A FREE MAKEUP CASE

NO RISK GUARANTEE:

There's no obligation to buy — the free gifts are mine to keep. I may preview each shipment for 15 days. If I don't want it, I simply return the books within 15 days and owe nothing. If I keep them I will pay just $12.50 (I save $2.50 off the retail price for 6 books) plus postage and handling.

"I'm trying to help you, Rafael, but you've got to help me."

He turned his head and exhaled a heavy stream of cigarette smoke. "You have all the help you need, Leah."

She was accustomed to the cryptic way the Gypsies often spoke, but she was lost now. "I don't know what you mean. I have so little to go on. I went to the jewelry shop today and discovered that a few days before she died Sheila had been looking at a man's signet ring with the initial M. Do you have any idea who she could have been thinking of buying the ring for?"

He shrugged. "No. Why did you go to the jewelry shop?"

She touched the pearl necklace that hung from her neck and fell over her breasts. "Because the clasp was in danger of falling off."

He nodded as if he understood, and drew on his cigarette.

"Rafael, you told me the night Sheila was murdered that your affair with her was over."

"It had ended last summer."

"Then why did she want to meet you at the cabin?"

"To say good-bye."

"You mean because you were leaving?"

"No. Because she was."

"She was going someplace? Where?"

"I arrived too late to find out." He drew hard on his cigarette. "She looked so pitiful. I couldn't stand the thought of her lying there all night by herself. I called myself all kinds of fool, but . . ."

"You phoned and told them where to find her, didn't you?" The nod he gave was a barely discernible movement of his head. "Then do you have any idea who the person was who called to say you were at the scene of the crime? And if he saw you, did you see him? Rafael?"

He leaned his head back against the wall and fixed his gaze on the small, barred window set high above him. "I can see a bit of blue during the day and a patch of black at night. But they won't open it so that I can get air."

He had told her all he was going to. She shifted along the cot and lay her head against his chest. "Somehow, some way, I'm going to find out who murdered Sheila, and then you'll be free. I promise."

His hand came up to tenderly hold her head and he placed a gentle kiss on her hair. Then he returned his gaze to the window.

Leah spied a large pebble nestled in the grass not too far from where she sat with Stephen beside the lake. They had walked from town to this shaded, grassy spot after she had convinced him to leave his car behind, and during their walk she had relayed her conversation with Rafael. She reached for the pebble. "Either he doesn't know anything or he does know something but he's keeping it to himself."

"Why would he do that?"

"I don't know. He said I have all the help I need, and I have to have faith that he's right. Rafael and

Zarah are very wise, and he will be king of his tribe one day." She threw the pebble into the water and watched as the ripples spread in ever-widening concentric circles until they disappeared. "I just wish I knew what he meant."

"Tim McCafferty showed me the first page of the crime report," he said, "and you were right. Rafael gave no last name and a check of his fingerprints turned up no previous criminal record and therefore no last name."

"Rafael wouldn't have a record because he's not a criminal. And, anyway, it doesn't matter that we don't know his last name. Sheila wasn't thinking of buying that ring for Rafael. There was someone else in her life. She had asked him to come to the cabin so she could say good-bye. She was going to run off with someone, someone whose last name begins with an M. If I could just figure out who that person is . . ." Something he had said struck her. "Why did Tim show you only the first page?"

"Evidently that's all they'll show without a court order, and the first page gives only the name of the victim, the victim's address, date of birth, and approximate time of the crime."

Stephen was beginning to get intrigued with the murder, although, he admitted to himself, he wouldn't have the slightest interest if it weren't for Leah. His lips curved at another thought. And he certainly wouldn't be sitting by a lake in the middle of a workday if it weren't for Leah. It seemed his life had become a circle where everything led back to Leah. And he liked it.

His eyes followed the progress of a sailboat as it glided over the silver-gray water, its sails tilted to catch the wind. There was no one around them, and the only noise he heard was the chirping of birds. He waited for Leah to speak again. When she didn't, he looked at her and found her watching the sailboat. "It's nice here. I'm glad you suggested this."

"Zarah says life needs time to happen."

He gave what she said some thought. "I guess that makes sense . . . in a strange way."

She turned to gaze at him. "Is it really true that everything you've ever done has had reason and logic behind it?"

He grinned at her obvious amazement. "My father owns a chain of hardware stores in Massachusetts, and growing up, I spent a lot of time in those stores." Her expression of puzzlement made him go on. "Nothing makes more sense than a hardware store. Everything is bright and shiny with its own place and fits together perfectly with something else."

"But you have to find the something that the something else fits with, right?"

"Yes."

"And what happens if you find the wrong something else?"

"Then you keep looking until you find the right something else."

"And you never give up."

He shook his head.

"That's the problem with most people," she said

thoughtfully. "They find a bad fit, and instead of looking for something that will make it work, they throw the whole thing away."

"Is that what happened with you, Leah?"

"Yes. More or less. My mother . . ."

"Tell me."

"No. Not now, at any rate. Tell me more about when you were a little boy."

"Well, I studied a lot. I shadowed my father around his stores. I broke my arm once when my bike crashed into a neighbor's fence. I got into the normal amount of trouble." He shrugged, at a loss to know what she wanted.

"Tell me about your mother."

"She's a very nice lady. She's going to love you."

Leah doubted that, but didn't say so. "When I was six, the Gypsies took me. The only reason my mother came to get me was that she was afraid she'd get in trouble if she didn't. Besides, with me gone, she didn't have anyone to blame things on."

"My mother's not like that."

The sympathy she heard in his voice grated her nerves. "What's your favorite color?" she asked abruptly.

Once he recovered from his surprise, he laughed. "Why all the questions?"

She was silent for so long, he wasn't sure she was going to answer him. But finally she said, "The night we met, I decided it wasn't necessary to know anything about you. Now I know differently."

"Then I'm getting through to you."

Her smile was wry. "Definitely. And you really shouldn't be. I haven't made up my mind yet how much is you and how much is the pearls."

It no longer bothered him when she said something he didn't understand. He reached over and took hold of the necklace. "Why are you so hung up on these pearls?"

"Zarah gave them to me the night we met. She said magic would follow. It has."

"That night *was* magic," he said, his voice soft. "Along with every minute I've spent with you since. But you make the magic, Leah, not the pearls. The magic is *in* you."

She shook her head, feeling suddenly defenseless. "You don't understand."

"You're wrong. This is one thing about you that I understand perfectly." Still holding the necklace, he let his hand rest lightly against her breast.

Her lips tightened even as her pulse raced. "What's your favorite color?" she repeated.

He recognized the question for the evasion it was. "I don't know. I guess I've never thought about it before."

"Think about it now."

"All right." He considered the matter, then smiled. "My favorite color is all the colors you make me see when we kiss."

"That's not fair," she said on an indrawn breath.

His hand moved over her breast, brushing down over the nipple, then skimming upward to her throat. "If I play fair with you all the time, I may never get what I want. And I want you."

It seemed as if his hand were touching every intimate part of her body, when in reality he'd merely grazed his hand over her sundress. But he had her craving more. "I'm beginning to believe you were absolutely right when you said we may be nothing but ashes by the time this is all over with."

"Damn, Leah."

He reached for her, but she drew away. "No, Stephen, I'm—I'm sorry, but I'm . . ."

His hand closed into a fist. "You're not ready. I know. It's been the problem all along. That and the fact that I'm too ready."

Backed by the blue sky, his eyes showed a clear, deep forest green. For a moment she felt she could read every emotion he was feeling, and amazingly she realized she wasn't frightened by what she saw. "I don't want to deceive you in any way, Stephen. I may never decide that I'm ready. My life, my past, your life . . . There are too many differences between us."

"None that matter."

"It's been my experience that people think differences are very important." She shrugged. "Anyway, right now I have to concentrate on helping Rafael."

He was barely able to stifle his impatience. "It doesn't sound like Rafael wants help."

"He wants help desperately. Every hour that he's locked up takes an hour off his life."

Stephen gave a deep, resigned sigh and gazed down at his still-clenched fist, resting on his upraised knee. Slowly he relaxed his hand. "Okay. Okay. What next?"

She studied him. He was a man clearly out of his element, yet it didn't seem to bother him. He was caught up in magic and didn't realize it. He was involved in a murder investigation and knew neither parties involved. He was trying to understand her, and she was trying *not* to understand him. He made her heart beat fast and her lower limbs heat, and he said he wanted her.

"You should go back to Dallas," she said quietly.

His head came up. "Dallas has lost all interest for me. It has no colored lights."

She bit her bottom lip. He really was smart. He said things in a way that resonated within her. Anytime now, it would cease to matter whether or not she thought she was ready.

"About what we should do next," she said slowly. "Sheila's best friend was a woman named Dorian Brown. I think we should talk to her."

He heard the *we* and was satisfied. "Let's go then."

Dorian and Sheila had been two years ahead of Leah in school, both of them pretty and popular and with no time for an insecure younger girl. Both of them had entered into loveless marriages. Dorian had become a hard, discontented woman, and Sheila had been murdered. It would seem her life had turned out the best, Leah mused. Still, she found it extremely difficult to question Dorian.

And to make matters worse, she had the feeling that if Stephen hadn't been with her, Dorian wouldn't have invited her into her home.

Firmly grasping the end of the pearl necklace, she swallowed the huge lump in her throat only to have it come right back up and interfere with her words. "I was . . . uh, wondering . . ."

"Yes?" Dorian was posed in front of the pink marble fireplace in her living room, unwilling to take her eyes off Stephen.

"First let me say that I know that you and Sheila were best friends, and I'm sure her death has been a terrible shock to you."

"Shock," Dorian agreed. "I've heard about your new home, Stephen. I'd love to see it sometime."

His answer was a pleasant smile, but he reached over and took Leah's hand.

His gesture had a calming effect on her. "Did she tell you she was preparing to leave town?" Leah asked.

The question jolted Dorian and switched her attention to Leah. "How did you find out about that?"

She instantly decided on an evasive answer. "You weren't the only person she told."

Dorian shook her head in disgust. "The little fool. First of all, I tried to tell her that after the grand passion faded, Gary wouldn't be able to make her happy. But do you think she listened?" Leah went still. Oblivious to Leah's reaction, Dorian rushed on. "Then I told her, for heaven's sake, keep your plans quiet. Maybe you can leave town with a few things, you know . . . by the time Robert misses them, you'll be long gone."

Dorian obviously believed she knew who she was talking about, Leah realized. Possible ways in which she could get Dorian to say the man's last name flew through her head, but she was unable to settle on one.

"Gary?" Stephen asked Dorian in the polite, puzzled tone of a newcomer to the town.

"Gary Mercer. Can you believe it? Sheila was willing to throw away her life for someone who draws a salary, and a *teacher's* salary at that. He couldn't offer her one third of what Robert could. I told her—"

Stephen pulled Leah to her feet. "Thank you very much, Dorian. It's been a pleasure meeting you."

Five

Honest, grief-stricken emotions were displayed on the handsome face of Gary Mercer as he sat talking with Leah and Stephen on the front porch of his small house. "I loved Sheila. I was willing to give up teaching, move to a strange city and start all over again. And now"—his voice broke—"it's all over. She's gone, and I can't . . . I can't believe it."

As Leah listened to Gary, she decided he couldn't have murdered Sheila. His pain was palpable. She'd felt an awful sinking sensation when she'd come to the conclusion that Robert Donaldson hadn't killed his wife, but for Gary Mercer, she experienced only sympathy.

And the question remained: Who had killed Sheila?

"Did anyone besides Dorian know of your plans?"

He swiped at his eyes. "No, of course not. Robert Donaldson is a prominent man in this town. Neither Sheila nor I wanted to be around when the scandal about us broke. We planned to leave separately, meet up in Dallas, and then decide where we'd go from there. We didn't care where we ended up as long as we were together and far away from here."

"When did you plan to leave?"

"The next day, that is, the day after she was . . ." He cleared his throat and now his expression turned accusing. "She planned to tell the Gypsy, Rafael, that very night. She asked him to meet her at Robert's fishing cabin—Robert was always too busy to use it—and that's where she and I met whenever we could. I didn't like the idea of her meeting with the Gypsy, but she insisted that he had been there for her during a particularly rough time last summer when the carnival was here." He hesitated, his expression hard to read. "She admitted to me that they'd had an affair."

Leah wasn't sure what to ask next. She threw Stephen a helpless glance.

He stepped in right on cue. "Are you absolutely sure that Sheila's husband didn't know about your affair with her?"

"Positive. As I said, he's a busy man, what with his business and his position in town and all. He largely ignored Sheila, except for those times when he'd verbally beat her black and blue." He shook his head. "I can't believe she's gone. We were so close to happiness . . . so close. . . ."

• • •

Stars blazed in the night sky above Leah's head, and the breeze whispered through the pines, scenting the air with a sweet freshness. The night had an innocent feel to it, she thought. A good feel. Yet Gary Mercer sat all alone in his small house, grief-stricken, Zarah waited in the Gypsy camp for her son to be released from jail, and somewhere a murderer felt satisfaction that he had gotten away with killing Sheila. Leah's hands tightened on the railing that edged Stephen's backyard deck.

Stephen had taken her to see Zarah after they'd left Gary's house and had stayed in his car while she visited with her. She hadn't been able to offer any comfort to Zarah regarding Rafael, but strangely she had been comforted simply by being with the woman who loved her like a daughter.

"Can I get you something more to eat or drink?" Stephen asked, coming up behind her.

She turned to him with a smile. "No, but thank you. I'm not accustomed to being waited on."

"It's entirely my pleasure." He pushed at the sides of her hair so that its lustrous brown length fell behind her shoulders. "I'm not sure who I have to thank for getting that grill for this house, but I'll have to find out. I'm getting pretty good at grilling."

"Are you telling me that last night was the first time you'd ever cooked on a grill?"

"That's right, but there's really nothing to it. In fact, the whole process is very logical. You get the briquettes hot, put on the steaks, pork chops, or whatever, watch them to make sure they don't burn, then take them off when they're done."

She snapped her mouth shut. "Is everything so easy for you?"

"Not everything," he said, gazing at her. "But most things."

"Then you're very blessed."

"In many ways," he agreed, "but I've also had to *make* a lot of those blessings."

She shook her head in disagreement. "I'm sure you leap over obstacles with a single bound."

"It's more like I use the hand-over-hand method of climbing to get over those obstacles. And along the way, some purchases I reach are easy, some aren't."

She regarded him thoughtfully. "I'm well aware that I haven't asked you a lot of questions about yourself," she said slowly. "And under the circumstances, I suppose my lack of questions has been a little unnatural. I don't know. I think perhaps it's been an unconscious act to protect myself."

"You don't need protection from me," he said softly. "I would never hurt you."

"Maybe not deliberately."

He curved his long fingers around the back of her neck and rubbed at the taut muscles he found there. "Not in any way, Leah. Besides, you know quite a bit about me. I think you instinctively *feel* a lot about me. And you understand that having you love me as I love you is my greatest ambition."

Tears welled in her eyes, and she blinked them

away. His words made a part of her feel warm and wonderful inside. So why did she have to fight those feelings, she wondered with despair. Why did there have to be a part of her that was constantly and terribly frightened to reach out for happiness? "What I understand is that up until two days ago, making a profit was your greatest ambition. But you'd conquered the mountain of business. Then you saw me and you saw a new challenge."

His eyes glinted with gentle admiration. "You really know how to go straight to the heart when you want to, don't you?"

Standing so close to him, her sundress provided no shield against the rising heat of his body. She wasn't sure why, but she was so attuned to him, she could measure his growing need inside her own body. She brought her hand between them and grasped the pearl necklace. "Am I right?"

"Yes, Leah, you're absolutely right. To a point. The night we met, I was restless. I'd discovered that trying to relax when I really wanted to work eighteen hours a day was very irritating. I was driving my boat fast to try to get the restlessness out of my system, when the carnival drew me. That's when I saw you and everything that is you—stillness, colored lights, fear and laughter, beauty and sadness. And I saw the most intriguing challenge of my life. It didn't make sense. It completely baffled me, but suddenly I was perfectly happy to be where I was. Suddenly I fell in love."

Scared and very fragile, she broke away from him and put the width of the deck between them. "That's not true."

He folded his arms across his chest, staying where he was. "Why don't you think so?"

"Because . . ."

"Ah, because."

"Because . . . it just isn't true."

He studied her for a moment. "You want to know what the real reason is? You won't *let* yourself believe, Leah, which I find rather amazing. You believe that your pearl necklace is magic when it's really just a piece of jewelry, very lovely and probably very valuable, but still just a piece of jewelry. You believe that your friend Rafael is innocent when all the evidence says otherwise. Yet you won't believe I love you. Why is that?"

"*Because,*" she replied, angry and tormented, "it doesn't hurt anything to believe this necklace might carry magic. And it can only help Rafael for me to believe he's innocent. But if I let myself believe you love me, then I'd have to rearrange every thought I'd ever had."

He smiled. "But, Leah. You've already begun to rearrange your way of thinking. You're simply not ready to face the conclusions you're reaching."

His smile and his gentle persistence worked on her anger, diffusing it. "You're right," she said in a small voice. "And I don't want you to be right."

He slipped his hands into the pockets of his slacks and started toward her, keeping his pace slow and unthreatening. "All you have to do is accept, Leah. Accept that I love you."

Warily she followed his movements as he crossed the deck and stopped in front of her. "I can't do that," she said softly. "Because I'll hurt too much the day I realize you don't love me."

Stephen bowed his head, experiencing his own pain. No matter how hard he tried, there was still a part of her he couldn't reach, a self-contained, cautious, fearful part of her, and he didn't know what to do about it.

She sensed his suffering and was at a loss. The gentle breeze tangled in her hair, caressed her face, and whispered in her ear. She heard Zarah's voice speaking of the stars, wisdom, and peace. She heard Gary Mercer saying, "we were so close to happiness . . . so close."

Her gaze locked with his, and a portion of her resistance gave way. "I can do one thing," she said. "I can accept the fact that I love you."

His whole body jerked. "You love me?"

She nodded solemnly.

To his dying day he would remember this moment, he thought. But to him the next moments were equally important. The touch of his hands was light on her shoulders, even though the muscles of his body were burning from being held rigid with iron control. "And what's it going to take to prove to you that I love you and won't ever leave you?"

"Does it matter so much that I don't believe?"

"It matters one hell of a lot."

Her brow wrinkled. "Can't you just take what I can offer? It's a lot."

"Actually, Leah, to have you say that you love me means everything to me. But I want things perfect between us, and perfect means that you accept that I love you. Until you do, we can't plan a future."

She almost gritted her teeth with frustration. "Stephen, listen and try to understand. You may be used to having things perfect in your life, but I'm not. There are too many elements of my life that are flawed, too many people who are depending on me for their livelihood. But I've discovered and admitted my love for you, and that love is like a bright corner of my life. You're here with me now. You've been with me through interviews with people that would have been unbearable for me without you. You've stood beside me regardless of your feelings about Rafael's guilt or innocence. You've looked at me and made me feel as if I'm very precious to you. You've touched me and made me feel as if I'm the most beautiful, most desirable woman in the world. And you've made me love you and want you. For now, take what I can offer you. The future—well, the future is just too unpredictable. But there's tonight. Let's take it."

"Damn, Leah, you don't make things easy." His hands tightened on her shoulders. "And you make them too easy."

"I'm *trying* to make them easy. Did you hear Gary Mercer? He and Sheila were so close to happiness, and in one horrible moment it was all taken away from them. Tonight is being offered to us. We need to accept or we might not be given another chance. Kiss me, Stephen. Please kiss me."

He trembled as he brushed his lips across hers and felt his control evaporating into the pine-scented air around them. "If I start kissing you, I won't be able to stop this time," he muttered. "Are you sure that's what you want?"

"I want you."

"How I love you, Leah, and one of these days soon, you're going to know it too. But until then . . ."

His mouth pressed roughly against hers, but his arms around her were compellingly tender. To him, the kiss was a summation of all the feelings that had been growing between them and a portent of what was to come. He had the tremendous, almost unbearable urge to try to possess her. But a thread of sanity told him that possessing Leah would be impossible. Instead, he'd wrap her around him and become a part of her for a little while. He'd absorb her colors into him. And when it was over, he'd care for her and do everything in his power to make sure she had no pain. And then he'd make love to her again.

Her arms went around his neck and her fingers threaded into his hair. Desire came crashing down around her like a heavy, driving rain of fire. She reeled with its force and clung to him, savoring everything that was Stephen, and everything that together they made each other feel. Then the time to savor passed, because all too soon she found herself ablaze, dissatisfied, and yearning for what her body was telling her could be. She dragged her mouth from his and dipped her tongue into the dimple in his chin, then ran a line of kisses up his jawline until her lips were against his ear. "I don't know how much longer I can stand."

He shuddered. "Let's go into the house."

"No. I want our first time to be outside beneath the stars." Her words were breathless.

"But—"

"Don't you have a quilt or something?"

"Leah—"

"I want you *and* the stars."

"I'll be right back." He tore away from her and disappeared through the kitchen door.

She'd gotten her way, but without his physical support, she was left swaying like a delicate flower in a strong wind. The red skirt of her sundress pressed against the heated need of her thighs, and a strand of hair blew across her sensitized lips. She felt buffeted by need, aroused beyond reason.

Within a minute he returned with the comforter from his bed. "This doesn't match a thing," he said. With her hand in his he led her down the steps of the deck and onto the lawn. At the edge of the woods he spread out the quilt and brought her down onto it with him.

Their clothes soon were in a pile to one side; the pearl necklace was laid carefully on top of the clothes.

The grassy lawn and the comforter cushioned them. The moon and the stars provided their light.

The passion and sweat of their bodies and the needles of the pine trees made the perfume.

Poised above her, he looked down and said, "This will be the first time I've ever actually made love."

Then he entered her with exquisite tenderness, and made himself a part of her. Sweetness and primal cravings looped and swirled and knotted within them until they created new colors and redefined the height of the sky.

Pale light filtered through tall, undraped windows as Leah awoke in a huge bed wrapped in Stephen's arms. A sense of contentment and happiness to which she was unaccustomed filled her. She turned her head and studied the soft thick cinnamon-color lashes that rested over the hard cheekbones of his face. Such a man of contrasts, she thought. He could be so gentle with her, so patient, yet he had planned to sell the radio station without seeing it, taking jobs away from people without ever meeting them. And he probably still planned to sell it.

Why had he come into her life, she wondered. Could their meeting have been just a coincidence? Or had their love been directed by the magic of the pearl necklace? Did the necklace *really* have a special power? Or was its power held within her belief in its power?

She sighed. She supposed she should view the matter as she would a superstition. Maybe it wouldn't hurt anything to walk beneath a ladder. But why take the chance when there was an alternate route?

The lashes raised, and dark green eyes looked at her with a lazy seductiveness.

"You have beautiful eyes," she said, and lightly ran her hand over his night's growth of beard.

He smiled. "And you're beautiful all over."

She felt herself turn pink. "I feel marvelous. Rested. Tingling. Strange."

He chuckled and gathered her tightly against him. "All of that, huh?"

"All of that and more. It's shameful. I need to get up, but I don't want to."

"Then don't."

He rose on one elbow, curved his hand around her breast, and covered her mouth with a languid kiss. A fire kindled inside Leah and grew as the kiss intensified and his hands explored her body, searching for and finding the highly sensitive spots he had learned so well last night.

She began to move against him, and he responded with a hunger that took her breath away. He stroked and touched her until she was writhing beneath him, senseless with passion.

Then, incredibly, he paused and looked down at her. "You taste like morning and flowers. I love the way your body feels to my hands, and I love the way I fit into you."

Her eyes widened as she grasped the significance of his words. "We do fit, don't we?"

"We fit so perfectly that when I'm inside you, I

never want to leave. And when I'm not inside you, like now, I want to be."

Her throat clogged with desire, but slowly the glow in her eyes died. "It's utterly impossible."

"Convince me, Leah."

She uttered a sound that combined passion and anguish, wrapped her arms and legs around him, and drew him into her. "Not now."

Wearing the pearls and the red sundress she'd had on the day before, Leah walked around the lake, her head bent, her thoughts disturbed. When they had awakened after their morning's lovemaking, Stephen had told her he needed to make some phone calls.

For several days now she'd had him all to herself, and she felt jealous and threatened that he was communicating with what she'd come to consider his other life—even though she'd told herself a hundred times that their relationship had too many complications to survive. It was just that his almost constant presence beside her had been so easy for her to accept. But now it was brought home with full force that he was an important man with a demanding business and a whole different life back in Dallas, complete with friends and other relationships.

She hadn't been able to stay in the house while he made the calls, and despite Stephen's protests, she had insisted on taking a walk. Running a length of the pearls back and forth through her fingers, she tried to convince herself that everything would be all right. She failed.

"Leah, my dear, what an extraordinary necklace."

It took a moment for the words and the voice to jell in her mind. Then she looked up into the face of Jane Scoggins, the woman who had recently retired from a thirty-year career as Sunnyvale's high school English teacher. "Miss Scoggins. What are you doing here at the lake this morning?"

"Just out for a little constitutional, my dear. Every year it gets harder and harder to convince myself to exercise. The necklace is simply lovely."

"Th-thank you."

The tall, heavily built woman lifted the necklace and studied it through her bifocals. "Not everyone can wear pearls, you know. Some women have too much acid in their skin. Ruins the luster. But these pearls have a wonderful sheen. You must agree with them." She dropped the necklace. "How have you been, my dear? You're doing a bang-up job at the radio station. Listen all the time. Of course, there's not much else to do when you're retired." She paused from her clipped, fact-filled, instructorlike way of talking to draw a breath.

"Thank you," Leah quickly inserted.

"You were one of my brightest students. I wish I were still teaching, but the school board has this stupid rule about retirement. Getting old is the very pits. Youth is everything. Enjoy it while you can." Miss Scoggins sighed with regret. "I guess I'd better turn around and head home. I can walk only so far at a time. I envy Gary Mercer."

The name brought Leah's wandering mind to attention. "Gary Mercer?"

"He *jogs*. Routine as clockwork. Jogs past my house about ten most nights, then turns around at the end of the block and heads back up the street. I can't get to sleep before one or so in the morning, so I sit in my front room and sew and see him every night at ten. Of course, there was the other night when he was jogging at midnight." She shook her blue-haired head, baffled. "Where does he get his energy? And that night he just kept right on going toward the lake."

"He came this way? Do you remember which night that was?"

"I'm old, my dear. I can't sleep like I used to be able to. And I never could jog, but I can still remember." She gave a cluck of her tongue. "Besides, it was the night poor little Sheila Donaldson was killed. Terrible tragedy. Maybe I made a mistake in not jogging when I was younger. Of course, young ladies didn't run back then. Well, good-bye, my dear. It was nice seeing you. Keep up the good work at the radio station."

"Good-bye, Miss Scoggins."

The tires of Stephen's car kicked up gravel as they rolled to a stop in front of Gary Mercer's house. Gary was on his front porch, a beer in his hand.

"It's a bit early for him to be drinking," Stephen said as he switched off the car's engine. "And he doesn't look too pleased to see us."

"It can't be helped. On our last visit I let my sympathy for him cloud my judgment. All I was concerned with was whether or not he'd killed Sheila. When I decided he hadn't, I forgot to ask him one important question." She opened the door, but right before she stepped out, she glanced back at Stephen. "Do you think I could have been wrong about Gary? Do you think he could have killed Sheila after all?"

"All I know is that someone killed Sheila. If it wasn't Rafael, and we don't think it was Robert, then that man up there on the porch has got to be a suspect, and he could have had any one of a dozen motives. Maybe he and Sheila argued over Rafael. Maybe at the last minute she'd gotten cold feet about leaving town with him."

She nodded and got out of the car. "Good morning, Gary."

"What do you want?"

He'd had more than one beer judging by the belligerence in his tone, she reflected as she made her way across the small yard to the porch steps. She noted Stephen's presence behind her with gratitude. He hadn't blinked an eye when she had burst into his study and practically dragged him to the car. "I need to ask you a question, Gary."

"I won't talk about Sheila, if that's why you're here. It hurts too damned much."

"You want her murderer caught, don't you?"

His eyes and voice were dull. "He's already been caught, Leah. Everyone in town knows that but you."

Stephen's hands closed warmly around her arms to reassure her. Unconsciously she leaned against him. "Gary, I need to know if you were at the cabin the night Sheila was killed."

His face twisted and he took a deep guzzle of beer. "Yeah," he said softly. "I got there, saw that Gypsy leaving, went in, and found her lying on the floor. I didn't even have to touch her to know that she was dead." He held up a helpless hand. "I couldn't seem to take it in. I mean, I'd seen her at the carnival just a few hours earlier. She'd been so happy, so alive. Then she was lying there . . ." He looked away, his teeth clenched against his grief. "I just couldn't cope. I ran."

She eased away from Stephen and climbed the steps to the porch. Laying a hand on Gary's shoulder, she knelt beside his chair. "Why did you go there in the first place? Had she asked you to meet her there?"

"No, not really. Because of the carnival, I jogged later than usual, and I decided to run by her house to see if she was back from her meeting at the fishing cabin. The garage door was up and the garage was empty, so on impulse I jogged out there to see her."

"Have you told the sheriff any of this?"

He took another swig of beer. "I saw no reason to get involved and every reason to stay out of it. She was dead and so were our plans. No one knew about us. I figured I had to go on living and working in this town . . . somehow." His voice faltered. "I was too broken up that night to do much of anything except get home. But the next morning I made an anonymous call to the sheriff's office and told them Rafael had been there. I decided I should do that much." He glanced down at her, an angry expression on his face. "I also told the sheriff about Sheila's affair with Rafael. It's my guess that he went into a rage and killed her after she told him about us. It's the only thing that makes sense."

But it *doesn't*, Leah thought.

Six

Sitting on her bedroom floor with her legs crossed, Leah stared at the pearls she held in her hands. She'd come home to shower and change, and she now wore an off-the-shoulder cotton dress of deep turquoise.

"Leah," Stephen asked, "what are you doing?"

She glanced up. He sat relaxed in the big lounge chair she'd upholstered in a hot pink corduroy. He looked good there, she thought absently. "I'm fretting."

"Fretting?"

"It's the pearls. Ever since Zarah gave them to me, it's like they've been leading me."

"You're imagining things."

"No, just listen." She tossed the pearls onto the bed and scooted across the floor to him. "I'll skip the part about you and me, because . . . well, just because. What I'm talking about now is how the necklace seems to be drawing me through a maze of untruths and truths toward the killer."

He shook his head. "Leah—"

"*Think* about it, Stephen. I went to visit Robert because he seemed the most likely suspect and found a dead end. The next morning I really had no idea what I should do. But then I discovered the clasp on the necklace was in danger of falling off, and I had to take it to the jeweler. It was there we were offered the fact that Sheila had been looking at signet rings, and that fact eventually led us, through Dorian, to Gary. He also seemed like a dead end, until this morning, when Miss Scoggins stopped me to admire the necklace and she let drop a remark that sent us back to Gary."

"But we didn't learn anything. Well," he amended, "we did learn that Gary made the second phone call to the sheriff. That could've been an attempt on his part to cast guilt on Rafael, but that's certainly not anything we can take and run with."

She chewed on her bottom lip. "I don't know. It seems to me that the pearls keep pointing to him. I feel there's something significant buried in what he said that I'm just not grasping."

"Honey, do you have any idea how strange that all sounds?"

Her brown eyes were very grave as she looked up at him. "To you I'm sure it does. But even with your logic and need to make sense of things, you must admit that life holds many mysteries."

"I admit it, but—"

"The night we met, Zarah reminded me that I had been exposed to the mystic ways of the Gypsies for many years. I guess that's why I can believe."

He reached down and pulled her up so that she knelt on her knees between his legs. "If only you would believe in you and me."

She smiled softly. "Ah, well, you and me. We're certainly something that seems to *be* at the moment, aren't we?"

"That's right," he said eagerly, "and what we feel for each other cannot be disputed."

Her smile slowly faded. "Remember the tilt-a-whirl we rode?"

"Of course I do."

"I feel I've been on it ever since, spinning and going up and down. Everything's blurred, yet at times things are so clear it hurts to look at them."

He groaned. "Leah, you're a fabulous creature. If I put the stars, moon, sun, rivers, and sky together, maybe I would have your mind."

Not knowing what to say, she put her arms around his neck and hugged him fiercely.

When at last she drew away, he threaded his fingers through one side of her hair and lifted the mass away from her face. "I've got something that I've been putting off telling you."

All the softness in her body disappeared as she tensed.

"Hey, it's not that bad," he chided gently. "It's just that I've got to drive back to Dallas today. In fact, I should have been on the road an hour ago."

The old feelings of fear and anxiety threatened. She got to her feet, went to the center of the room, and gazed blindly around her.

He was immediately beside her. "It's not even noon yet. It'll take me two hours to drive there. I'll spend a few hours in the office, and I'll be back this evening."

"It's all right. Really." She wrapped her arms around herself, warding away the cold and the withdrawal. "I know you have responsibilities. I've known all along. It was only a matter of time."

He took her in his arms and cradled her close. "I said I'll be back this evening, and I will. I'm not leaving you. I'm simply going to Dallas to see to some things." With a tender smile on his face he spoke softly and rubbed her back with caressing, soothing circles. "You haven't told me a lot, but I've been able to figure out certain things for myself. And one thing is very clear to me—you've had so much rejection in your life, you're afraid to let yourself see how much I love you. But I do love you, Leah. And I will always come back to you."

She listened carefully and discovered that she wanted with all her heart to believe him. And perhaps, she thought, *wanting* to believe was the first step toward actually believing. Warmer now, she pulled back and looked up at him. "I'll miss you."

"Come with me."

She shook her head. "I can't. I need to talk to Zarah."

He hesitated. "Will you be all right?"

"Why wouldn't I be?"

"I don't like the idea of you pursuing this investigation all alone. It could be dangerous."

"If you think that, then you believe the murderer is still walking around free, while Rafael sits in jail for something he didn't do."

He grinned. "You have a very persuasive way about you."

She wasn't satisfied. "*Do* you think Rafael is innocent?"

He sighed. "I haven't seen any hard, cold facts to support his innocence, but yes, I guess I do think he didn't murder Sheila."

A glow of happiness settled over her face. "That's good. And I *am* going to miss you."

"You'd better," he said, and ground a kiss onto her lips.

As always, being with Zarah in her tent gave Leah a sense of well-being. No candles had been lit yet today, but the sun filtered through the gold-colored fabric of the tent, gilding everything including the two women who sat side by side on the daybed and the dress that lay across Leah's lap.

She gazed down at the creation with amazement and delight. The strapless bodice was a haze of spangly magenta stars. The skirt was drifting silk panels of magenta, pink, and fuchsia. "You've never made me such a beautiful dress before."

"I wanted you to have something special."

"This is more than special, much more. I love it. I can't imagine anything more gorgeous."

"And there are high-heel shoes that match." Zarah's tone implied she was well satisfied with Leah's pleasure.

Leah chuckled. "And you're the one who taught me the joys of going barefoot."

Zarah lifted her shoulders and let them fall. "Sometimes there are events . . ."

"I don't know what it would be. I never go anywhere where I could wear something like this."

"That is not a matter over which you should be perturbed. An occasion will present itself, I am sure."

"But, Zarah, you shouldn't spend your money on me like this."

"*Bah.* You are my child. I shall make you clothes if I choose. Now let us speak of why you are here today." Zarah smiled. "You have come to ask me about the pearls, have you not?"

Leah felt no surprise at Zarah's precognition. "I don't think you've told me everything you know about the necklace."

"You are right."

"But why, Zarah? Why have you kept it from me?"

"Because we were waiting for the pearls to do their work."

"We?"

"We, the Gypsies, are descendants of a nomadic tribespeople. Who's to say where we first started? Who's to say who we really are? It is not important that we know."

"What is important?"

"The pearls. They have been with us for over twenty-five hundred years. But not continuously. They disappear for long periods of time, yet when there is trouble for our people, the pearls always appear. So when the pearls showed up this time, we knew to prepare for trouble."

She knew better than to discount what she was hearing, but still . . . "You mean you just turned around one day and the pearls were there?"

"Yes. And one day they will disappear again."

"And you knew the necklace was here to help you?"

"It is our history."

"That's incredible." She gazed down at her lap, where the bottom loop of the necklace lay pooled on top of the magenta stars. The pearls and the stars appeared to gift each other, the stars receiving a glowing iridescence from the pearls, and the pearls drawing a slightly deeper color of pink from the stars. A sudden thought occurred to her. "But why did you give the necklace to me?"

"Because, my child, you have a pure heart, and we consider you one of our own. We knew that you would help us if we couldn't help ourselves. When Rafael was put into jail, we knew we had been right. We were outsiders in this town. No one would tell us anything. Besides, a Gypsy has no chance in a white man's court. You were the only one who could help us."

"I don't know how much help I've been, Zarah. I've discovered certain things, but I'm not sure

I'm any closer to finding out who killed Sheila than I was the day I started."

She patted Leah's hand. "You should not be concerned. I am not. Neither is Rafael. The pearls will do their work."

"I worry about him. He is losing his spirit in that place."

"But he knows that soon he will be free."

"I wish I had your faith."

"You have all you need. You are attuned to the mysticism of the universe even if you are not aware."

Leah grimaced. "Stephen would tell you that I'm too attuned. Poor man, I drive him crazy."

"Stephen? Ah, the cinnamon-haired man of whom you've spoken."

Uncertainty entered her dark eyes. "Zarah, about Stephen . . . You made a prediction for me when you gave me the pearls, and it seemed to come true. The night I met him I felt different. Since then my life has changed both in little ways and in big ways. And there's the unalterably and amazing fact that I've fallen in love with Stephen. But I have to know how much the pearls have to do with all of this."

"It is up to you to decide."

"*Zarah.*"

The old woman held up a hand. "No, I have said all I can."

"All you can or all you will?"

Zarah smiled slowly. "Again, my child, that is up to you to decide."

• • •

"It's working," Pat reported gleefully. "Our revenues are up. The new management has got to be impressed now."

"You've been doing a great job, that's for sure," Leah said, studying the reports on the accounts Pat had acquired over the last few days. "I'm glad I decided to stop by the station."

"Margaret told me about that awful man. The accountant," she added when Leah looked at her in query. "She said he wasn't in here long at all, and we couldn't decide if that was good or bad."

"That makes three of us," Leah said wryly, then went on in a more serious tone. "I don't really know what to tell you on that subject. As you know, I've been very preoccupied with trying to find something to help clear Rafael of Sheila's murder. But as soon as Rafael is free, I plan to present these new figures to . . . to the management. I just hope he, I mean, the management, thinks they're as impressive as I do. And in the meantime, I've been given the impression that TCIC won't take any negative action."

"Well, that's something, at any rate. You know, I've been pleasantly surprised by the response I've gotten. The people of this town have heard about the TCIC buy, and they don't want to lose the station any more than we do."

"It's gratifying to know that people are enjoying what we're doing here."

Pat wiggled in her seat, then sat forward. "I can't stand it any longer. I just have to ask."

Leah chuckled at the avidly curious expression on the younger woman's face. "I can tell you right now, I don't have any answers."

"You'll be able to tell me this, because it's about that necklace. I've been hard pressed to keep my eyes off it, much less my hands. It's gorgeous. Where did you get it? Did you buy it somewhere, or did someone give it to you? If you bought it, how much was it? I mean, could I afford one? And if someone gave it to you, for goodness' sake, tell me who." Suddenly Pat grinned and drew in a deep breath. "Will you listen to me? I sound like I'm filling out a crime report. You can sure tell I'm dating a deputy sheriff, can't you?"

Leah stared at Pat. "That's *it*. Good heavens, why haven't I thought of it before?" She shoved the phone across the desk so that it was within easy reach of the younger woman. "I need you to do me a big favor."

The hinges creaked as Leah pressed her foot against the porch and propelled the swing back and forth. She didn't know how long she had been sitting there, her gaze fixed firmly on the road that ran in front of her house, but she did know that it had been dusk when she'd come out on the porch and now it was night.

Stephen will be here, she told herself. He said he would return tonight, and he will.

Headlights brightened the horizon. Leah's pulse leapt, but the headlights flashed quickly by and disappeared down the road. He'll come, she thought, and had no idea why she felt such confidence.

Absently she picked up one of the pearls and rubbed it between her fingers. If only Rafael weren't in jail. But she was close to the truth. She could feel it. Hopefully if everything went well tomorrow, she would have her answer.

Another pair of headlights appeared. The necklace dropped from her fingers and settled against the turquoise bodice of her dress. Forcing herself to remain calm, she watched the car decrease its speed and turn into her driveway. The Mercedes pulled to a stop in front of her house, the engine cut off, the door opened, and Stephen stepped out.

Leah leapt from the swing and launched herself off the porch toward him.

Laughing, he caught her to him. "I said I'd be back."

"I've been waiting for you."

"Have you?" He pressed a kiss to her lips. "I would have been here sooner, but there was a traffic tie-up on the interstate coming out of Dallas. On the way to Sunnyvale I decided I should buy a helicopter."

She drew back in horror. "Oh, no—"

"It sure would be convenient. It would cut my commuting time to—"

"But you'd be *flying*!"

He smiled down at her. "Bad idea, right? Okay, I'll forget it, for now, at any rate." He glanced up at the house. "No lights?"

Bewildered, she followed his gaze. "What?"

"You didn't turn on any lights."

"It never even crossed my mind." She took his hand and led him up the stairs and onto the porch. Pulling him down beside her on the swing, she asked, "Do you have to go back to Dallas tomorrow?"

"No. I'm set for a few days." He paused, afraid that what he was about to say was going to bother her. By the dim light of the moon he could make out her features, but he wanted to be able to see every nuance of her expression. "Why don't we turn on a few lights?"

"Why? It's so peaceful."

"Peace is inside you, Leah. Not around you."

She thought about it. "That's not always true."

He got up and flipped on the porch light, then sat back down. "I've gone an awful long time to-day without seeing that lovely face of yours. Do you mind?"

She grinned. "How could I when you put it that way?"

He placed his hand along her jaw and tilted her mouth up to his. He tried to hold back his pas-sion and fill the kiss with a pure love that would bolster her in the next few minutes. His strata-gem worked only to a point, and then desire be-gan to take over, pulsing through his veins and reminding him of how very much he wanted her. He broke off the kiss and gently stroked her face. "I have some good news."

"What's that?" Her dark brown eyes softly gleamed with trust and love.

"I talked to several of my friends this afternoon, and they reminded me that I had planned to throw a housewarming party as soon as the house was complete." He felt her stiffen and deliberately gave a light chuckle. "They actually threatened me. They said they'll be down Friday night, with or without an invitation. So I guess we're throwing a party night after next. It'll be fun, don't you think?"

Leah couldn't answer. The familiar fear and anxiety closed in on her and left her paralyzed.

Stephen skimmed his fingers from her face to her bare shoulder, feeling the clamminess of her skin. "I know you're worried about Rafael and probably don't feel like a party, but you won't have to do anything other than show up and have a good time. My secretary is contacting everyone, and I'll hire a catering service to handle all the work." He infused humor into his tone. "And, naturally, I'll use a *Sunnyvale* caterer. I've learned my lesson."

Leah willed normalcy back to her body. Didn't Stephen understand? She truly believed that the only reason she'd allowed herself to fall in love with him was because he hadn't known her and hadn't had any preconceived ideas of her. That and the pearls . . .

But now his friends would be coming, and he wanted her to meet them. She'd spent years being an outsider in a town populated by people probably just like his friends. What if these people he obviously admired and felt affection for saw that she was different? What if they treated her as an outsider? Would he think less of her then?

Her chest was tight, breathing was difficult. Her hand urgently clenched around the pearls.

"Leah? I'm touching you, but I'm not reaching you. You're withdrawing and I refuse to let you. Talk to me. Tell me what's wrong."

She took several deep, shaky breaths until her lungs once again had life-giving air going in and out of them. "Your friends are all sane," she finally managed. He looked at her oddly, and she went on. "The night we met, you said that everyone you know is sane."

"They're very nice people."

"I'm sure they are," she said with grave doubt.

He took her arms and swiveled her body in the swing so that she faced him. "I'm not going to lie to you. I could have stopped them from coming. In fact, I almost did. But then I realized that it would be good for you to meet my friends. You have it so firmly fixed in your mind that there's this huge chasm of experiences and life-styles between us. And I can't deny that we're bringing diverse elements into this relationship. But that just makes it all the more interesting, and it's wrong to look at these things as something to overcome. Because of the different things we know, we can learn from each other and create a rich, full life together."

"You really believe that, don't you?"

"Yes. And I won't stop until I can make you believe it too."

She stood, walked to the edge of the porch, and leaned her shoulder against one of the supports.

Her heart still beat erratically, but at least she was breathing more easily. "I guess the least I can do is try."

He came up behind her and rested his hands on her shoulders. "You're wonderful," he said. Having gotten her to agree to what he wanted, he decided it best not to dwell on the upcoming party. "I'm hungry."

"You're always hungry," she murmured dryly.

"Just at mealtimes, which you tend to forget. Would you like to go get something to eat? Or we could drive to my place, and I could throw something on the grill."

"I'd rather stay here."

"Okay then, I could run to the store and—"

"No.' She turned her head and looked at him over her shoulder. "I want to sleep alone tonight."

His brow creased into a frown. "You're not withdrawing from me again, are you?"

"No. I just need to be alone tonight."

"Leah—"

"Please, Stephen. Try to understand, this has nothing to do with you."

He wanted to argue. He wanted to stay and hold her close all night long, to reassure himself that she had not withdrawn from him. But her set expression convinced him he wouldn't be able to change her mind. Reluctantly he gave in and left.

And Leah spread her quilt beneath the midnight-black sky, pulled around her every particle of peace she could grasp, and slept.

Seven

Tim McCafferty opened the back door to the jail at Leah's knock and nervously checked the alley behind her to make sure no one was about.

"For goodness' sake, Tim, let me in."

He cracked the door only wide enough to let her slip in, then closed it with a sigh of relief. "No one can know that you're here."

"I understand, and I really appreciate this."

"The only reason you're going to get a look at that crime report is because Pat asked me. I could lose my job. Do you know how many laws I'm breaking?"

"Not really, but as I said, I really do appreciate it. And do you suppose you could get me a cup of coffee? At six A.M., my body demands caffeine."

"Leah, for heaven's sake, just read the report and *leave*."

"Okay, okay. Where is it?"

He motioned for her to follow him into a small, unused office and pointed to the desk which was bare except for a brown folder. "Stay in here and keep the door closed. I'll come get you in ten minutes."

She sat down behind the desk, pulled the file toward her, and began reading a detailed description of what the police had found when they'd arrived at the cabin. The description noted the position and condition of Sheila's body, and the state of the room in which she had been discovered. Apparently the room was in order. The report also listed the spilled contents of Sheila's open purse that was found beside her: a compact, comb, lipstick, car keys, cleaner's receipt, checkbook, and a small package of tissues. Nothing unusual, Leah concluded. A dust for fingerprints had turned up four sets: Sheila's, Robert Donaldson's, Rafael's, and one set that was unidentified. Gary Mercer's, Leah thought, and turned to the statement that indicated a search of the area around the cabin had turned up nothing. Lastly there was the coroner's report and a set of photographs of the body.

She closed the file, sickened by the clinical account and the gruesome pictures, just as Tim came back into the room. "I brought you a cup of coffee," he said, handing her a paper cup of dark, steaming liquid. "I hope you take it black."

"That's fine."

"Did you find anything that you can use to help your friend?"

She shook her head. "I don't know. It all seems so cut and dried, but I can't help thinking that there's something obvious I'm missing."

"It seems a pretty open-and-shut case to me, Leah. Maybe you should save yourself a lot of grief and accept the fact that Rafael killed her."

She pushed back from the desk and stood up. "Thanks for the coffee, Tim. And thanks again for bending the rules."

"*Bending?* Leah, I broke them clean in two." All at once a shy grin broke out over his face. "But I'd do anything for Pat. She's terrific, don't you think?"

Leah smiled. "I sure do."

Outside in the alley again Leah automatically headed around the side of the building. Sipping her coffee, she went back over what she had just read, putting it together with what she had learned previously.

At the front of the building she turned the corner and headed toward the lake. What *was* it that was nagging at her, she wondered. There was something that was staying just beyond the reach of her mind, something that if she could only get hold of it . . . she completely lost her train of thought as she collided with Robert Donaldson.

"Watch out! *Dammit,* look what you've done."

She gazed in horror at the coffee stain spreading over the front of his white shirt and gray suit. Her hand flew protectively to the pearls around her neck, but no coffee had splashed on either them or the blue dress she wore. "I'm terribly sorry. I wasn't watching where I was going."

"That was obvious. Now I'll have to go home and change."

She straightened with composure. "I said I was sorry. And if you'll send me the cleaning bill, I'll be glad to pay for it."

"You can bet you will. What are you doing here so early anyway? Visiting your Gypsy friend?"

She eyed him coolly. "I was just out taking a morning walk."

He glanced toward the building and back to her. "Well, I'm here for a purpose. I want to make sure that there are no hitches in getting that bastard convicted. The sheriff has been dragging his feet on charging him, and I want to know why."

"Have a nice day, Robert." She turned on her heel and headed for the Gypsy encampment.

She spent the morning visiting with Zarah and talking out the information she had gathered while Zarah offered tea and reassurance. But Leah was able to garner no new insights, and beneath Zarah's confidence, Leah detected an increased anxiety over Rafael.

Leah made her way to the radio station with a heavy heart. When she entered the station, she found Margaret beaming. "That nice Mr. Tanner is in your office."

An alarm bell went off in her head. "What's he doing in there?"

"He asked to see the books, and after he explained who he was, I gave them to him." The sight of Leah's pale face made her add, "I hope that was all right. I mean, he owns the station, and he does seem so nice. Lots nicer than that other person who came from Dallas."

"Don't worry about it, Margaret. You did fine. I'll go see if he needs anything else."

She walked toward her office, a cold feeling in the pit of her stomach. When she opened the door, he looked up from the accounting books spread over her desk and smiled. "There you are. I've been waiting for you."

"So I see." She closed the door behind her.

He rose, skirted around the desk, and met her in the center of the room. "Where were you this morning? I went by your house, and when I found you gone, I decided to come here."

"I just came from Zarah's. Earlier I was at the jail."

"Visiting Rafael?"

She shook her head. "No, reading the crime report."

"Really?" His eyes narrowed. "Should I ask how you got to see it?"

"You definitely shouldn't."

"Okay, then. Did you find out anything from the report that can help Rafael?"

"Unfortunately, no."

"I'm sorry."

"I am too." She walked around him and eyed her desk. "Stephen, I wish you'd told me you were going to do this. I was under the impression we had a tacit agreement." She turned to look at him. "I mean, I thought we were going to put this aside for the time being until I could get Rafael out of jail."

"It's all right, Leah."

"*No*, it's not. These books don't tell the story. For one thing, they're not up-to-date. For another, we have new accounts—"

"I'm not selling the station."

"What?"

"I'm not selling the station. That possibility completely vanished as soon as I saw how much KSUN meant to you."

She waved her hand toward the desk in silent bewilderment.

"Since I had the time, I thought I'd look into my newest acquisition. I think my interest was natural, don't you? To tell you the truth, I didn't care what I found. If there was more red than black, TCIC would have simply used KSUN as a writeoff, and you could have continued on as you had been. But I discovered that you've been doing a great job. I also talked with Margaret and the fellow in the booth, Harry Morrison."

"Harry talked to you?"

Stephen nodded. "He told me how much this job means to him, and how grateful he is to you for giving it to him."

"Really? He's never said anything like that to me."

He regarded her thoughtfully. "You've really done

a remarkable thing here, Leah. You've employed people who for various reasons were unable to fit in anywhere else, and in the process you've given them a sense of self-worth and usefulness. I admire that."

On some barely conscious level she'd wanted desperately to do just what he'd described, but she hadn't been aware of exactly what she'd accomplished until she'd heard it from him. His words meant everything to her. She blinked away the tears that stung at her eyes. "I have to ask you something."

"Anything, you should know that."

"Are you keeping the station only because of our relationship?"

He took his time in answering. "Yes."

She clasped her hands tightly together and looked down at them.

With a knuckle beneath her chin, he raised her face. "You want me to be honest with you, don't you? If it hadn't been for my caring so damned much for you, I would never have even seen this place, much less talked with Harry and Margaret. Those are simply the hard, cold facts of my business."

"Then let me ask you another question."

"All right."

"When . . . if our relationship ends, what will you do about the station?"

"Always expecting the worst, aren't you?" he asked softly. "Well, then let me put your mind at ease. I have seen the station. I've even listened to it. And I've talked with Harry and Margaret. There's no way I'll sell the station as long as I know it's operating the way it is now."

The relief she'd been suppressing surged forward. "Thank you, Stephen. You're a remarkably nice man."

His eyes held laughter, but his handsome face expressed indignation. "You're just now figuring that out?"

She angled her head and regarded him thoughtfully. "I recognize that you've been very gentle with me. I suspect you saw you had to be. But I also recognize that you have another side. You have a smile that reminds me of a shark. Granted, I haven't seen it since that first night, but I'm sure you can flash it in an instant."

"One way or the other, Leah, you keep me constantly amazed. That's quite an analysis. And very accurate. Regarding the station, there's one more thing you should know. Sometimes my business decisions are hard as hell to make, but this one was a cinch. It made perfect sense. And regarding you, I love you very much, and while gentleness and patience don't come easily to me, with you it's a cakewalk."

A lovely smile melted away her serious expression. "And there's something you should know. I wouldn't have fallen in love with you if I hadn't seen your basic niceness. Just don't use that shark smile on me, okay?"

"Okay." He brought her to him and held her

close for a minute. "Why don't we go have some lunch?"

"There you go again with the food."

"It's time for another meal. My bet is you skipped breakfast."

"Yes, well . . . There's a little café we can go to that serves a really great steak sandwich. On the way there I'd like to tell you what the report said and get your opinion. Maybe you'll be able to see something I'm missing."

"That's a good idea. My car's out front."

"Why don't we walk?"

He rolled his eyes at the suggestion of walking. "I'm hungry. Let's take the car."

On the way to the café Leah related in detail to Stephen the contents of the crime report. She explained about the condition of the room, the fingerprints they'd found, and the position of Sheila's body. She mentioned Sheila's purse with its spilled contents. She even went into the coroner's report with him.

He threw her a glance as he pulled into the parking lot of the café. "That must have been hard for you to read. I wish you'd told me you were going there this morning so that I could have gone with you."

She leaned against the door and shrugged. "Tim would have been doubly nervous with both of us there. *Oh*—I ran into Robert Donaldson outside the station. Literally." She grinned. "Spilled coffee all over him."

"Was he awful to you?"

"He was angry, but then, I'd just ruined his shirt and suit. And he's still angry at Rafael. He said he wanted to make sure nothing went wrong. He doesn't want him to get away on a technicality, and I'm sure he intends to try to press the sheriff into charging Rafael."

"Let's go in and toss what we know back and forth. Maybe it'll help."

"I hope so. I feel like there's something staring me right in the face." She shifted so that she could grasp the door handle, and somehow the rope of pearls hooked on the handle. She automatically tried to pull them free, but at the same time she straightened, causing the tension on the pearls to tighten.

"Oh, damn."

"What's wrong?"

"It's the pearls. They're caught on the door handle."

He chuckled. "Relax. The car doesn't want your pearls. Just lean forward—"

She went still. "The car . . ."

"What?"

"I told you the pearls kept pointing to Gary— that I felt he was saying something significant I wasn't grasping." As quickly and as carefully as she could, she freed the pearls, then, excitement gleaming in her eyes, she turned to him. "It's the car."

"The car?"

"Gary told us that he jogged by Sheila's home, he didn't see the car, and decided to go to the lake. Now, though he didn't say it outright, it seems to me his actions imply that he believed she *drove* to the cabin. But the crime report said that they found nothing around the cabin—surely they would have mentioned her car—and her car keys were in her purse. Don't you see?"

He nodded slowly. "If her car wasn't in the garage, and it wasn't at the cabin, where was it?"

"Exactly."

"Could Robert have driven it to work?"

"They have a two-car garage. Gary said the garage was empty. That means both cars were gone."

"Okay, then we'll assume she drove to the cabin."

"Then someone had to drive the car away from the cabin after she was murdered."

"Why afterward?"

"I can't imagine anyone stealing a car in Sunnyvale, but even if someone did, Sheila would have heard the car start up and gone out to see what was going on. Then she would have been killed outside."

He regarded her levelly. "You're sure about that?"

She looked doubtful for a moment. "I haven't heard anything about Robert filing a stolen-car report."

"Would you have heard?"

"Well, under normal circumstances, yes, I would. KSUN has a local news report. But I have to admit that I've been out of touch."

"So maybe he has filed a report."

"Let's go ask him."

He stared at her. "Now?"

"Now. He'll be at his office. I'll show you which way to go."

"Sheila's car is sitting at home in the garage," Robert Donaldson said implacably. "Where did you ever get the idea that it had been stolen?"

"Because it seems to be unaccounted for the night Sheila was murdered."

"You're mistaken. The car was in the garage the whole night."

Stephen spoke up. "How do you know that? You were here."

Robert's eyes were hard and cold. "Sheila often walked to the lake. Besides, the car was in the garage when I got home. If you think that it was someplace else during the murder, then I suggest you talk to the bastard who's sitting in jail."

Leah sat forward in her chair and leaned her arm on the desk. "Robert, your wife has been killed. It's all been horrible for you. But if there's the slightest doubt that Rafael killed her, that means that the real murderer could be walking around free. You don't want him to go free, do you? Don't you want to make sure that the right man is tried and convicted?"

"But I'm already sure that's going to happen." His fist came down hard on his desk. "Leah, for God's sake, if you hadn't been practically raised as one of those filthy Gypsies, you'd see that Rafael killed Sheila. He has been placed at the scene of the crime and the jewelry that Sheila was wearing that night was found in his trailer. What the hell more do you want?"

She stood her ground, pale but steady. "I want to find the person who murdered your wife. And I'm going to do exactly that, with or without your help."

Robert pushed back his chair and jerked to his feet, his face red with anger. "Then it's going to be without my help, because let me tell you something—I've cooperated with the sheriff, and I've spoken with you twice now, answering every one of your stupid questions, but this is where it ends. I'm fully aware that people around here considered that Sheila and I had a bad marriage, but I never did. Now she's gone, and I have to deal with that fact as well as the brutal way she was murdered. The sooner I pull my life together and go on, the better."

"I understand—"

"You can't even begin to understand. And if you bother me again, I'll turn you in to the sheriff for harassment. Now get out of my sight."

The file drawer shut with a metallic clunk, and Sheriff Johnson turned back to Leah and Stephen. "You've been mighty busy, Leah."

She'd told the sheriff about Gary and Sheila's affair after deciding it was important that he know.

"No one else in this town believes that Rafael is innocent. I've had to be busy." She hesitated, but received no response. "Gary said the garage was empty. Robert said the car was there. I think it's significant to know exactly where it was."

He eyed her thoughtfully. "What made you latch onto the idea of the car?"

Unwilling to jeopardize Tim's job and tell the chief that she had seen the report, she hedged. "It just struck me as odd. Doesn't it make you wonder?"

Stephen spoke up. "One of the men is obviously lying. The trouble is, their outrage over Sheila's death seems very real, and then there's the problem of motive. Do you think Robert might have known about his wife's affair with Gary Mercer? If he did, that would sure give him a motive."

The sheriff shook his head. "I've known him a long time. Why, he was one of the best quarterbacks Sunnyvale High ever had. He played cards with me and a few of the boys the night before Sheila was killed. Trust me. He never had a clue. He didn't know about Rafael until I told him the next morning, and he sure as hell didn't know about Gary. Hell, *I* didn't even know, and I generally know everything." He settled his large frame into the chair behind his desk with a disgruntled expression on his face.

Leah squirmed with impatience. "But will you question Robert and Gary?"

"Robert became very angry with Leah," Stephen

explained, "and said he didn't want to see her again."

"Can't say as I blame the man. After all, his wife has been murdered, and to top everything off, he's found out she'd been having an affair with a Gypsy." He shook his head regretfully. "Now I'll have to tell him about Gary."

"Sheriff, we all feel bad for Robert," Leah said. "And for Sheila. And *I* feel bad about Rafael, if no one else does, because he's innocent. Now I've asked you to do something that's nothing more than your job. Will you?"

The sheriff sighed heavily. "All right, Leah. You've made your point. I'll check into the now-you-see-it-now-you-don't car, but I'll tell you this much, I don't think it'll amount to a hill of beans. When I went to tell Robert about Sheila that morning, both cars were in the garage. And I will let you in on one fact. Her car was not at the cabin. My money is that Gary made a mistake."

"But he seemed so sure. As a matter of fact, that wasn't even something I asked him. He just let it drop very casually."

"I'm not saying he was lying. In these sorts of circumstances, you've got to remember the setup. It was dark, he was running down a street that's not that well lit, and he glanced up at the house and *thought* he saw an empty garage. The door could have been down, and from his position on the street he just misinterpreted what he was seeing." The sheriff spread out his hands. "An honest mistake."

Leah's hopes that she had discovered something that would free Rafael took a dive. Nevertheless, she persisted. "You said you'd check—"

"Like a dog with a bone, aren't you? Don't worry, Leah. I'll talk to both men and let you know what I find out."

"Thank you."

Rafael's black eyes had grown dull, and his brown skin held an unhealthy pallor. Leah ran her hand down his cheek with a loving caress. "It hurts me to see you locked up like this."

"I need to leave this place," he said simply.

It was the closest he'd come—or would come—to breaking down in front of her, and she felt helpless to comfort him. "Trying to find out who really killed Sheila has been the hardest and most important thing I've ever done, and I'm not sure I've made any progress at all. Every time I think I've discovered something, it turns out to be a dead end."

"Perhaps one of those dead ends will open up soon and show you the way."

"Is there anything else you can tell me, Rafael?"

"Just this one thing. You have great strength, and you have the pearls. You will succeed. I trust you."

"About those pearls," she began.

He drew her to him, and cradled her against him with arms and hands still powerful no matter the state of his spirit. "Zarah has told you all you need to know. Now I want to hear about the man with the cinnamon hair."

"He's wonderful. I love him. And he says he loves me, but . . ."

"Pretty little girl," Rafael murmured softly, threading his long fingers through her hair, "you've known so much hurt in your life, you can't bring yourself to believe that lasting happiness might finally be yours."

"Rafael is a tough man," Leah told Stephen later on that night as they sat out on his deck. "But keeping him locked away as they are is a crime against his soul. He tells me not to worry. Zarah tells me not to worry. But they and all the Gypsies are worried. There has been only melancholy music being played in the Gypsy camp the last few days, and there has been no dancing."

"Let me get Rafael a lawyer. I'll bring in the best I can find."

"Rafael wouldn't allow it."

"Then let me hire a team of investigators. They'll scour this town until they find something."

"They'd find nothing because this town would close up tighter than a nuclear submarine."

He grinned wryly. "So what's new? Sunnyvale hasn't struck me as open up to now."

"But we've learned things, and I think when we find out who moved the car, we'll know who murdered Sheila."

"I hate to say this, Leah, but what the sheriff said made sense."

"Maybe that's why I don't believe it."

"Okay, let's say you're right, and the car was moved. Let's come at it from another angle. Instead of *who* moved the car, let's ask *how* the car was moved."

She looked at him with interest. "That's a good question."

"Thank you."

"Sheila's keys were found beside her body, so whoever moved it didn't use her keys. Therefore, he or she would have had to use another set or hot-wire it."

"We've discussed the possibility of a car thief and dismissed the idea," he said thoughtfully. "But Robert would have had a set of keys to her car."

"That's right," she said, sitting forward, then had a thought that made her excitement drain away. "Or Gary could have hot-wired it."

"And as we've noted before, both of those men seemed to have been hit hard by Sheila's death."

She toyed with the pearl necklace. "I don't know. At the time I didn't think either of them was acting."

"I had the same impression, but guilt is a great incentive to act well."

"I realize that now, and one of them had to have killed her."

Stephen reached across the table and took her

hand. "Well, we've made progress. We've decided that the killer has to be one of two people."

She looked at him and said very quietly, "Have I told you lately how having you by my side has made everything infinitely easier." In one easy, natural motion, she rose from her chair and transferred to his, curling onto his lap and wrapping her arms around his neck. "Thank you, Stephen, for being with me through all of this."

"This was exactly where I wanted to be. All I had to do was talk you into letting me stay."

She smiled. "You were very convincing."

"Have I convinced you that I love you?"

She rested her forehead against his. Her silence lasted so long, Stephen began to worry, but he remained quiet and waited.

"I think I do believe," she said at last. "I'm just not sure *why* I do."

"Does it matter?" he asked, his voice rough and uneven as he tried to contain his happiness lest it frighten her.

She lifted her head away from his and looked down at the necklace she wore. In ancient times pearls were worshiped as moon symbols and harbingers of good fishing and safety on the water. No other gem seemed to hold such a powerful mystique. These particular pearls possessed a beauty that was magical. But were *they* magical? And if they were, what would happen if they were ever to disappear from her life . . . their life? She had no answer for either herself or for him.

"Will you stay with me tonight?" Stephen asked softly.

She nodded. "Out here."

Stephen placed quilts over a mound of pine needles for their bed, and together they lay down. Overhead, a soft wind whispered through the scented pine boughs. And they made sweet gentle love beneath the stars.

Eight

"I hate wearing the same clothes I wore the day before," Leah observed, wrinkling her nose at the dress she had had to put back on. She and Stephen were eating breakfast in the glassed-in sunfilled morning room that looked out over the lake. The water sparkled with light.

"There's an easy cure," he said with a smile. "Move all your things over here."

Her fork halted midway to her mouth.

He groaned. "I'm sorry, that was clumsy of me. But it can't come as a surprise to you that I want very much for us to be married."

Slowly she lowered her fork to her plate. "Let's don't talk about this right now."

He made an abrupt gesture. "Look, I'm making a mess of this, so I want to make sure you understand. A live-in relationship was not what I had in mind when I suggested that you move your things over here. It would be only a temporary measure so that we can be together while we decide what kind of wedding we want. Or, rather, what kind you want. I couldn't care less. All I want is you, and for the rest of my life."

"Stephen, I'm not ready."

"I don't understand," he said, momentarily thrown off balance. "Am I missing something? Last night you said that you finally believed that I love you."

She rubbed fretfully at her brow. "I do."

"And you've said that you love me. So what's keeping you from completely committing to us?"

"I told you. I'm just not ready."

He sat back in his chair and threw his napkin onto the table. "That doesn't make sense."

"I know."

The sadness in her voice made him all the more frustrated. But he had come to know her better than she thought, and he understood that at this point, pushing her would do no good. She had to come to things in her own way. The level of the coffee in his cup had lowered by half before he spoke again. "You're right. Now is not the time to talk about this. Rafael is still in jail. And there's the party this evening. I need to stay here at least part of the day. I have some work to do, and Mrs. Beacon and her people will have to be shown around."

Leah's eyes widened. "You asked Loretta Beacon to cater your party?"

"Well, yes. I inquired and was told she was the best. Why?"

She chuckled, feeling better now that the subject of their future had been dropped. "She's the *only* caterer in town."

"Is there something I should know? She seemed very enthusiastic when we talked yesterday, and she assured me that she'd create something really special for the party, but, now that I think about it, I have to admit that there was something about her that bothered me."

Leah nodded. "She's flaky."

"Oh, good, Leah, *now* you tell me."

"I don't recall you asking. But don't worry. She'll come through for you in the end. Loretta is a wonderful cook. It's just that she has this sort of inner catering muse that she listens to, and sometimes that catering muse leads her astray."

A look of foreboding came over his face. "Inner catering muse?"

"I think it's a very good idea for you to stay here and make sure things run smoothly. The last wedding she catered, she made six different three-tiered cakes before she was satisfied. They were all quite beautiful, I understand, but the wedding guests saw and ate only one."

"What happened to the other five?"

"We had a lot of fat, happy little birds around town that winter."

"Ah."

"Also the bride and her family had planned a sit-down dinner after the wedding. When they arrived after the wedding, they were confronted by an hors d'oeuvre buffet. When they asked her why, she replied that the crab hadn't spoken to her as a main course; rather, it had insisted on being an hors d'oeuvre."

"I'll stay here."

She laughed and got to her feet.

"Why don't you stay here too?"

Even though his tone was entirely casual, she didn't miss his concern. "Don't worry. For the moment, at least, I've run out of ideas. As much as I hate to, I've got to wait and see what the sheriff's investigation turns up. So I'll visit Zarah and then spend the rest of the day at the station."

He rose and took her into his arms. "Good. What time shall I pick you up this evening?"

She gave a groan of dread and buried her face against his chest.

He pressed a kiss on top of her head. "You're going to be surprised how easy this party will be for you."

"I'll bet."

"You're going to have fun, you'll see, because I won't give up until you do."

With a smile she tilted her head back and looked up at him. "And you never give up."

"Not about something I care about. Now, about that time . . . Everyone should start arriving by around seven, seven-thirty, somewhere in there."

"And you'll need to be here. Why don't I just make my way over by myself?"

"Oh, no. Not on your life."

"Do I detect a distinct lack of trust?"

"You detect a distinct and definite love."

She sighed. In the face of such sincerity she had no argument. "Then come over whenever you like."

Leah spent the day just as she'd told Stephen she would. But she couldn't keep her mind on any one subject or project for long. At four she gave up the effort and went home.

But once there, she couldn't relax. The coming ordeal of the party loomed large in her mind. She took a long hot bath and then gave herself a manicure. Finally, when she couldn't think of anything else to do, she got out the beautiful dress that Zarah had made for her and put it on.

Looking at herself in the mirror, she thought once again that she'd never seen such an incredible dress. The strapless bodice of star-shaped magenta-colored spangles glinted with reflective brightness. The magenta, pink, and fuchsia silk paneled skirt clung seductively to the curves of her hips, then floated in uneven lengths to around her knees.

She brushed her hair until it hung in dark glossy waves around her face and halfway down her back. Then she wrapped the pearl necklace once around her neck and let the rest of it fall down over the magenta stars to the silk skirt.

When she ventured a look into the mirror, she saw that the pearls had added their special magic to both her and the dress. *I'm beautiful*, she thought, and tentatively reached out to touch her image.

A great sense of relief flooded over her. Maybe for once in her life she would fit in.

It was Stephen's knock on the front door that brought her out of her reverie. And the stunned expression on his face when he saw her confirmed her expectations.

Delighted by his reaction, she laughed and circled the living room with a series of barefooted pirouettes. The silk-paneled skirt and the pearls swung outward, free of her. When she stopped, they wrapped around her body, embracing her, then slid back into place. "Zarah made the dress for me. Isn't it wonderful?"

"You're what's wonderful. You look like some earthbound angel encircled with colored lights. Come here."

She ran eagerly into his arms. He was wearing a dark brown suit, pale beige shirt, and brown, gold, and mahogany tie. He smelled vaguely woodsy, she thought, and very masculine. And suddenly she wanted him.

At the first touch of their lips the fire began. He groaned. "It's been a hell of a long day without you."

"I should have stayed with you," she agreed, and parted her lips for his kiss. A quick, hot response flooded her veins when their tongues met and tangled. The need was piercing and its intensity almost swept her away. Her arms wrapped around the back of his neck as she held on to him and centered herself in him and the feelings they were making.

Without asking, he unzipped her dress and took a step backward, relieving the pressure of their bodies to allow the dress to slide to the floor. Then he scooped her into his arms and turned in the direction of the doorway.

"What about the party?" she murmured, and glided her tongue along his jaw.

"We have time. Hell, we'll *make* time." He tightened his grip on her so that her breasts were pressed into his chest.

Suddenly she stiffened. "Wait, I don't want the pearls to get broken."

Stephen started for the bedroom. "To hell with the pearls."

She managed to get the necklace off and toss it onto a chair right before he strode out of the living room and into the bedroom. With her mind at ease regarding the necklace, she wrapped her arms around his neck. And when he lowered her to the bed, she didn't release him.

"I have to get these clothes off," he muttered, tortured by even the thought of the seconds he'd have to be physically parted from her.

"No," she whispered, agonized by the same thought as he. "Don't leave me." She kissed every part of his face she could reach, needing the taste, touch, and sensation of him.

"Leah—" Her lips came in contact with his mouth, and he gave up. He lowered himself to the bed beside her and kissed her with a hot, savage pressure. The heat that licked through him was scorching. He wanted more than anything to give her pleasure, but he wasn't sure he'd be able to. All he could think of was taking her as hard and as fast as he could, but she deserved such care. He tore his mouth from hers and closed his lips over the peak of her breast. "You taste like sugar and fire," he whispered hoarsely, and took a hard draw on her nipple.

It felt as if flames were eating their way down the center of her body to her thighs. Urgently she pushed at his jacket and without taking his mouth from her, he lifted slightly and slid out of the burdensome garment. Hungering for contact with his skin, she tore at his shirt and managed to separate it from the waistband of his pants. With a moan she spread her fingers across his back.

Her touch was almost too much for him. He slid his hand down her body to beneath her panties and found the wetness and the heat. His breath came raggedly as he stroked her.

She arched against him, and he pressed her back down with the heel of his hand. Her spasms of release began; he felt them and brought his lips down hard on hers. Soon she was cresting again, and her untamed response drove him to near madness. He thrust his tongue deep into her mouth time after time, but the act offered no satisfaction, and he knew he had endured all he could.

He unzipped his pants and entered her.

She cried out as exquisite pleasure bolted through

her with a violence that left her weak. He gave her his power, pushing it into her body until she twisted and bucked beneath him. And then they both went out of control.

She stirred and felt his arms around her. He breathed in and smelled the dark velvet-flowered scent of her and the fragrance of their mingled passion. Their lids fluttered up at the same time, and they stared into each other's eyes.

"I love you," he whispered, and stroked her face tenderly.

"I love you," she murmured, and kissed his fingertips.

"Whatever's bothering you, Leah, I'll wait for you to work it out. We have no differences that cannot be overcome. Do you believe that?"

"I want to, it's just that . . ."

Their eyes widened simultaneously, as they exclaimed, "The *party*." They rolled off separate sides of the bed and hit the floor running.

"Everyone's probably already there," he said, shoving his shirt into his pants and zipping them. "Run a comb through your hair, and I'll bring your dress to you."

Leah rushed to the bathroom to freshen up. Then, back in her room, she grabbed up the brush and pulled it through her tangled sable-brown hair.

Stephen dashed back into the bedroom carrying the dress. One look at her standing in front of her dressing table, naked except for a fresh pair of panties, and he groaned. "You need to put this dress on right away or we'll never get to the party."

She took the dress from him and slipped it on, knots tying and untying in her stomach. "The way I feel right now, that wouldn't be such a bad idea."

"I know you must be nervous," he said, helping her zip her dress, "but I'm going to be right there with you. They can't wait to meet you."

"You *told* them about me?"

"I love you, Leah. Naturally I wanted to tell my friends."

"Naturally," she said, her voice faint and carrying notes of doom. She turned back to the dressing table and hastily refreshed her light makeup.

Behind her, he finished straightening his clothes and retrieved his jacket. "Where are your shoes?"

She pointed toward the closet. "In there—the high-heel magenta ones."

He grabbed the shoes in one hand, her hand in the other, and pulled her out of the room. "Let's go."

It didn't take them long to reach the lake. Leah sat quietly beside Stephen, still slightly dizzy and disoriented from the incredible passion they had just shared. The party was going strong when he pulled his car into the driveway. A few of his friends were standing out on the front porch, and they waved and called to him. He opened his door, and Leah slipped out on his side.

Before starting up to the house, he bent and pressed a reassuring kiss to her lips, still slightly swollen from his lovemaking. "You look beautiful, Leah. In fact, I don't think I've ever seen anyone look more magical."

"Magical?" She went cold with horror, and her hand flew to her neck. *It was bare.* "Oh, no, Stephen! I've got to go back to my house! I left the pearl necklace there!"

He hesitated. "I know that necklace means a lot to you, but you don't need it. You look beautiful without it. I told you—"

She clutched at his arm, close to hysteria. "Please, just give me your car keys. I'll drive myself."

"Stephen," one of his friends called. "Come on up. We're all waiting to meet your Leah."

Watching her closely, he put his arm around her shoulder and drew her firmly to his side. "They've seen us. You can't leave now. Come on," he said, leading her up the path. "Everything will be fine. I promise."

Unreasoning and overmastering fear came crashing down on her and took her in its grip. Her chest went tight until she couldn't draw a breath. Her heart beat painfully and erratically. She searched frantically, but she couldn't find that still-peaceful place within her. She was totally helpless to escape the disaster that awaited.

On the porch, faceless people surrounded them. Stephen introduced her, but she heard no names. They said things to her, but she couldn't hear. And then they were inside the house. She blinked against the lights, but she couldn't see anything or anyone.

She needed the pearls.

Without the pearls she had no confidence or beauty.

Without them she had no magic.

"Leah, this is Jed and Sarah Kosta, two very good friends of mine."

Her hand was taken in a firm handshake. "It's a pleasure to meet the lady who did what every woman in Dallas has been trying to do for years— make Stephen Tanner fall in love," a deep male voice said.

A soft, lovely voice chimed in. "And you're just as beautiful as Stephen told us you were. We're delighted for both of you."

Leah's gaze slowly focused on a petite blond-haired woman who was smiling at her.

Stephen spoke again. "And this is Mary and Carl Harris. Carl cheats at poker, but otherwise I like him."

Carl Harris, a tall, brown-haired man, threw back his head and laughed heartily. "I absolutely do not cheat, Leah, but there are times I'd like to take the chair and break it over Stephen's head. He's too damned good."

Mary Harris, an attractive woman of about forty, grinned. "Carl and Stephen are both very compet-itive, but I'm sure you already know that about Stephen. I hope you don't mind us coming down like this, but once we heard about you, we couldn't resist. Please say you'll come into Dallas soon. I'd love to show you around."

"For heaven's sake, Mary, quit talking so I can ask her where she got that incredible dress." Leah's gaze switched to a cheerful raven-haired woman of about thirty-five. "Hi, I'm Jessica Blakemore, and if you tell me you can buy clothes like that in Sunnyvale, I'm moving here immediately."

"A friend of Leah's made it for her," Stephen said, "and none of you can move here. This place is my retreat, and I'm guarding it with my life."

"That's very selfish of you, Stephen," Sarah Kosta said. "Sunnyvale even seems to have a first-class caterer. The food and drinks are wonderful."

"Loretta and I decided on foods from the Southwest," Stephen said to Leah. "Nachos, fajitas, and the like, and I made her stick to the menu."

"Good food," Carl Harris echoed in his booming voice, "but I have to ask you about that ice sculpture over there. It looks sort of like a shrimp standing on its tail and wearing a sombrero."

Leah heard Stephen laugh. "That's what it is. Loretta is just learning to do ice sculpture. I figured if her inner catering muse was busy concentrating on the ice sculpture, she wouldn't have time to get creative with the food."

"Did you say inner catering muse?" Sarah Kosta asked.

"Tell me about your friend who sews such wonderful creations, Leah," Jessica Blakemore said.

Leah couldn't speak. Her throat burned with an awful dryness. Out of the corner of her eye she spied a waiter with a tray of drinks. With a stiff jerky movement she reached out, and her hand hit the edge of the tray, causing the tray to tip. The waiter took a step backward, trying to regain the tray's perfect balance, but to no avail. The drinks slid off and smashed to the floor, shattering the crystal glasses and sending various types of liquid flying.

"Are you all right, Leah?" Stephen asked urgently.

"I'm sorry," she managed to say.

"Don't be silly. There's nothing to be sorry for. Everything's fine. Let's just move away from this area so it can be cleaned."

As they walked to another part of the living room, with the six other people following them, Leah became aware that Stephen's arm had never left her shoulders since they'd entered the house. He'd told her he would stay by her side, and he was doing just that. But didn't he understand? She had to have the pearls. Tonight was going to be a disaster unless she went home to get them. She'd already managed to destroy a tray of drinks.

"Let me get you something to drink, Leah," Jed Kosta said. "What would you like?"

"Uh . . . ice water, please."

"Are you sure? Those boys over there at the bar are turning out some great margaritas."

"Ice water."

Leah jumped in surprise when the petite blond woman briefly squeezed her arm in sympathy. "Don't be nervous," she said softly. "Stephen loves you. That means we like you already."

Leah wet her lips. "Thank you. You're . . . uh . . . ?"

"Sarah. Sarah Kosta. And don't worry that you can't remember anyone's name. You'll be meeting a lot of new people tonight. We're only meeting one person."

"You're very kind." She turned to take the glass of water from Jed Kosta, bumped her hand against its side. Water sloshed onto his suit. "Oh!"

He laughed. "Now, now, it's only water, and it dries without a trace. Wish I'd invented it. Here, there's plenty left in the glass for you."

She took the offered glass and drank deeply of the cool water. Her throat immediately felt better. She cast a shy look around the group and felt Stephen give her shoulders a hug.

"I think I told you all that Leah is the manager of the local radio station here," he said proudly.

A chorus of yesses followed.

"I envy you, Leah," Jessica Blakemore said. "It sounds like a really interesting job. Oh, here's my husband. Darling, where have you been?"

"Just looking around." The slight, fair man held out his hand to Leah with a smile. "Hi, I'm Kirby. You have a remarkable face. I'd love to paint you."

Everyone laughed. His wife playfully punched his arm. "Kirby, you must learn to wait at least five minutes after meeting someone before you say something like that." Jessica turned to Leah. "I guess you've gathered by now that my husband is an artist."

"Of course," Leah murmured, "Kirby Blakemore. I've never been lucky enough to see one of your works except in photographs, but I think they're wonderful."

His eyes lit up with pleasure. "Then you will let me paint you?"

His wife punched him again. "It hasn't been five minutes yet. Stephen, I really like this bare look. No curtains. I think if I lived in a place like this, I'd do the same thing. We could tell as we drove up that you have a fantastic view."

Stephen answered Jessica, and Leah began to feel herself relax. It was true that she'd made some really awkward blunders, but these people still seemed to like her. She'd never once caught them looking at her as if she were strange. In fact, they were going out of their way to make her feel comfortable. Her hand went automatically to her bare neck. Maybe . . .

Her attention was suddenly caught by a man standing at the buffet table holding his throat, gasping for breath. Quickly she broke away from Stephen and moved toward the man. His eyes fixed on her, panic-stricken. Without saying a word, she moved behind him, placed her arms around him just below his rib cage, grasped her left wrist with her right hand, and exerted sudden strong pressure inward and upward. The man coughed, and a tortilla chip flew from his mouth.

"Are you all right?" she asked anxiously, moving back around him.

"Lord, how can I thank you?" he said, rubbing his throat. "I was scared to death. I thought I'd had it for sure. I couldn't get anyone's attention."

"I'm thankful I saw you. How do you feel now?"

The man nodded. "Fine, I think. I'll sit down though."

Stephen had come up behind her and he signaled to one of the waiters. "Get Mr. Dowell something to drink. Roy, do you think we should take you to the hospital?"

"No, and thanks to your lovely lady here, you won't have to take me to the morgue either. She was wonderful."

"You were," Stephen said softly, and kissed her cheek.

Several of the men went with Roy to sit with him. The women gathered around Leah.

"How did you know how to do that?" one asked.

She shrugged, amazed and pleased with herself. "I had read about the procedure, but I never knew if I'd be able to do it or not in a real emergency until I saw that man in distress."

The party continued. Stephen had hired several high school students who had their own band to play mariachi music, but they soon segued into soft rock, which was fine with everyone. Stephen's constant presence, plus the genuine warmth and friendliness of his friends, gradually put Leah at ease. So much so that late in the evening she'd relaxed enough to contemplate leaving Stephen's side, and she decided to go outside for some air.

"I'll be back in a minute," she whispered to him, and slipped from the circle of his arms.

Nine

A full moon was holding court over an absolutely clear night, Leah discovered as she made her way out back to the deck. Alone for the moment, she inhaled her fill of the pine-scented air, then smiled as she saw the small colored lights that had been strung around the railing.

She leaned her elbows on the railing and gazed back toward the house. The band was taking a break. Through the uncurtained windows she could see Stephen and his friends talking, laughing. They were a congenial group who seemed genuinely to like one another . . . and her.

Without the pearls.

True, she'd made some blunders, but anyone as nervous as she might have done the same stupid things.

"Leah."

A frown marred her smooth forehead. She turned to look toward the woods. Had someone just called her?

"Leah."

She peered through the moon-cast light to a tall, slim man standing at the edge of the woods. "Robert?"

He gestured for her to come to him. "I have some information that will help your friend."

She threw a hesitant glance at Stephen through the window.

"Come alone," he said. "I don't know any of those people, and I don't want to. Dammit, are you going to come out here, or am I going to leave?"

Her foot paused on the first step that led off the deck. "What kind of information do you have?"

"I know who killed my wife."

She wasn't blind to the danger of the situation. There was a fifty-fifty chance that *Robert* was the murderer. But for Rafael's sake she had to go to him and hear what he had to say. She would just need to be very careful. And it was reassuring to know that Stephen was just yards away, and if need be, she could run like the wind.

Robert was standing in front of a tall pine tree, and she stopped a distance that was halfway between him and the deck so that she was still visible from the house.

"Closer, Leah."

"I'm close enough. I can hear just fine." She saw his body change position, as if he might be thinking of leaving, and she quickly tried to distract him. "How did you know I was here?"

"Are you kidding? Loretta started broadcasting the news of the party as soon as she got the job."

"I see." Leah clasped her hands in front of her. "Okay, tell me. Who killed Sheila, because I know it wasn't Rafael."

"You're right," he said, his voice pitched low so that she had to take a couple of steps forward to hear him clearly. "But I sure as hell wish you weren't."

"Robert, you really didn't know about Sheila and Rafael, did you?"

He shook his head. "I told you, I considered our marriage good. When I saw her driving by my office that night, I had no idea where she was going."

"You *saw* her driving?" An excitement began to burn in the pit of her stomach. She'd been *right* about the car.

"I'd taken a little break from work and walked outside. I called to her, but she didn't hear me. So I got curious and jogged after her." He shook his head in disgust. "She'd told me she was going to stay home and do some needlework, and I'd believed her. I gave her everything she wanted. Everything."

Except love, approval, and respect, Leah thought, but didn't say it.

"When I realized where she was going, I got even more curious. I arrived at the cabin just a short time after she did, and I went in and confronted her."

He gave a low, harsh laugh that sent chills down Leah's spine and had her looking toward the house. A glimpse of Stephen bolstered her courage.

"Sheila was really upset to see me, and then she turned defiant. Said it was just as well that we have it out, and she told me about her and Gary Mercer. I couldn't believe it. I mean, I really couldn't *believe* that she'd been having an affair, and I hadn't even known it. God, I was furious. I told her she wasn't going to make a fool of me."

"It was *you*," she whispered, but he didn't hear.

"I took the two ends of that scarf and started pulling. I only meant to make her say she'd forget Mercer, but next thing I knew she was dead." He smiled crookedly. "You were so close to figuring it out, I knew it was only a matter of time before you did. Can you imagine, Leah, how shocked I was? My wife was dead, and I had *killed* her! To this day I have a hard time dealing with that."

He *hadn't* been acting, Leah realized, feeling as though her intuition had been vindicated. He had been stunned by the manner in which Sheila had died. And he hadn't known about Gary prior to that night. But only two things were important now. She needed to find out the rest of the story, and she had to lure him out of the woods. There was no doubt that the happenings of that night were a nightmare that constantly haunted him. He seemed obsessed with telling her the story. Maybe . . .

"If Sheila drove the car to the cabin, how did it get back to your house?" She took a step backward.

"Why did you have to figure out about the damned car?" he asked, almost snarling and taking a step out of the woods toward her. "It wouldn't even have occurred to most people to think of the car. I didn't for a while. You see, as soon as I realized Sheila was dead, I knew I had to leave fast. It seemed natural to take her car."

"But you didn't drive straight home, did you?" she asked, backing slowly.

His smile appeared eerily off balance in the white moonlight as unconsciously he drew closer to her. "You're very smart. But then, so was I. I decided to sneak the jewelry she was wearing into one of the Gypsy trailers. Everyone knows what dirty, lying thieves they are, and they were about to leave town. No one would have trouble believing that one of them killed Sheila for the jewelry."

The band had started to play again, making her aware that the music cut her chances of being heard if she screamed. She was also forced to raise her voice so that Robert could hear her. "How did you know which trailer was Rafael's?"

His lips drew back from his teeth in a laugh she could barely hear. "I didn't. Isn't it ironic? And so damned right. He deserves everything he's going to get."

Just a few more feet to the deck, Leah thought, taking two steps backward. He was following beautifully. "So then you drove home?"

He nodded. "And then I remembered that my

car was back at the office. So I jogged over there, taking the back way, of course, and got into the building without anyone seeing me." He was close enough now that she heard the laugh he gave this time, and it frightened her. "And right after I got there, I made sure the security guard saw me coming out of my office to get some coffee."

"You have to give yourself up, Robert."

"Why? You think confession is good for the soul?"

"You confessed to me."

"That's because you'll never tell anyone. Don't you understand? That's why I'm here. To kill you."

She wheeled for the deck, but she forgot to allow for her high heels, and one of the heels struck the forward edge of the step. Losing her balance, she fell forward. Robert grabbed her by the hair and yanked her upright. A sharp pain lanced through her head, and tears sprang to her eyes. She gave herself mere seconds to recover, then brought the spike of her high-heel shoe down hard on his instep. Robert let out a yelp, and his hold on her loosened. But when she tried to run, he snatched her back, wrapped her neck in an armlock, and began dragging her toward the woods.

Stephen was showing Jessica and Sarah the upstairs of the house and happened to glance out the window. His blood turned to ice at the sight of Robert Donaldson dragging Leah toward the woods.

Dear God, how was he ever going to get to her in time?

"Call the sheriff," he shouted to the two women, then sprinted for the stairway.

It had been a big mistake for her to think that if she stayed within sight of the house, she would be safe, Leah thought, engaged in the biggest fight of her life against panic and terror. But she couldn't die. She wouldn't. Not now, when the love and happiness for which she'd yearned all her life was about to be hers.

"Stop your damned squirming," Robert said, just short of the woods. He held her away from him, then brought a backhanded blow across her face. Stunned, she fell to the ground.

"You've got to die," Robert said, jerking her roughly upright and back to him. "Then everything will be all right. The sheriff will forget all about Sheila's death because he's got the Gypsy, and he'll never connect me with you."

Desperation gave her a surge of energy. Using all her strength, Leah jammed the heel of her hand upward into his nose. Both of his hands flew to his face. Blood gushed from his nose, and he dropped to his knees, crying out in agony.

Stephen rushed out the back door, down the stairs, and across the yard to Leah's side. "Dear Lord, are you hurt? What happened?"

She leaned against him, half sobbing. "Robert killed Sheila. He just told me everything."

He pulled her to him in a protective hold. All of the party had poured outside. "Take him out front and keep him there until the sheriff comes," he said over her head to two of the men. "Tell him Leah will be in tomorrow to make a statement."

She lifted her head. "Tonight," she said softly. "I don't want Rafael to have to spend one more minute than he has to in that awful place."

Stephen took her face in his hands, being careful of the mark already discoloring her cheek. "Are you sure you're up to it?"

"I'm sure."

Leah gave her statement, and in another room Robert broke down and confessed. When Rafael walked out of his cell, she was there waiting for him.

"Hello, pretty little girl."

She ran to him and his arms closed around her. For a long minute they were content in the happiness of the moment, then she drew back and smiled up at him. "I'm not so pretty. Did you see this bruise I've got on my face?"

A muscle moved in his jaw. "You have always been and will always be beautiful, Leah. It just makes me sick that you have so much as a mark of pain on you, and I grieve that you received the bruise helping me."

"I would have gone through much worse to help you."

He gently stroked a finger over the bruise. "What

you did was remarkable. You've finally realized the strength inside you. Now we must go tell Zarah everything that has happened."

Leah glanced over her shoulder at Stephen. "You go on. Stephen and I will be there shortly."

Rafael looked up at Stephen and slowly smiled. "That is a good idea."

In front of Leah's house Stephen turned the ignition key. He automatically reached for his door handle, but she stopped him with a hand on his arm.

"Let's just sit here for a few minutes. I need to catch my breath."

"All right." He studied her carefully. Other than occasionally touching her face, she didn't seem as if she felt bad. He wished she'd allowed him to take her to the doctor, but he decided to let the subject drop unless he noticed some sign that she felt worse. "I'm glad you wanted to be alone for a little while."

"So much has happened since we were last alone. I find it all amazing."

"I find you amazing," he said, and reached across the seat to draw her to his side. "You were wonderful tonight, but let me tell you something, if you ever put yourself in danger like that again, I'll . . ." Words failed him.

She smiled. "But everything worked out all right, didn't it?"

"Yes, thank heaven."

"Rafael is finally free as he was meant to be."

"Thanks to you and your persistence."

"You helped too."

"Not that much."

"More than you know," she murmured. "I was going to people for information, people who under normal circumstances I would never have had the courage to approach. And I was able to fight my way out of fear and anxiety attacks that only a few weeks ago would have sent me into full-scale withdrawal."

"You would have done the very same things alone. Look what you did tonight. You were clearly terrified, but you went into a party of strangers and completely won them over."

"They were nice."

"Granted. But their being nice or my being present didn't stop you from saving Roy Dowell's life."

She shrugged it off, even though she felt a glow of pride. "That was something I did without thinking."

"Exactly. And then you went out and confronted a murderer. He was going to kill you, but you put him out for the count."

"Not out for the count."

"You incapacitated him. Besides being in an incredible amount of pain, he couldn't see, and he couldn't breathe out of his nose. You did it all, and you did it without the pearls."

She stared at him. "You understood, didn't you?"

He nodded. "I knew you were confused about the pearls and Zarah's prediction and how they affected us. You'll never know the agony I went through when you asked me to take you back home. My heart told me to take you; my head told me to let you learn how wonderful you were on your own without the pearls. But I had faith in you. All I had to do was wait for you to learn to have faith in yourself."

"You were taking an awful gamble."

"Not really. I told you all along. The magic is in you."

"In us," she said softly. "In us."

He kissed her long and deeply, and despite the gentleness, the fire came. Leah relished the feeling. Yes, they would always have the fire, but now they also had their love, and the fire was stronger for it. It was with great reluctance that she ended the kiss. "The Gypsies will be leaving, and I want to say good-bye."

He smiled tenderly at her. "That's fine. We have the rest of our lives to kiss and to share the magic."

She leaned forward and briefly brushed her lips across his, silently agreeing with him. "Let's go inside for a minute. I want to see if I can cover up this bruise with some makeup. I don't want Zarah to be upset."

He nodded.

Inside, she passed through the living room on her way to the bedroom. But at the door to the hall she paused and looked back at the big easy chair. "That was the chair I threw the pearls onto before you carried me to bed."

He grinned. "Really? I didn't notice."

"But they're not there." She bent over the chair and ran her hands down the sides of the cushion. Then she lifted the cushion. "Where are they, Stephen?"

"Maybe they fell underneath it." Stephen shifted the chair out of the way.

She straightened, realization of what had happened dawning. "Stephen, the pearls have *disappeared*."

"I'll call the sheriff."

"No, wait." Staring down at the chair, she chewed on her bottom lip. "It's all right. Zarah told me that one day they would disappear again."

"Disappear? They've obviously been *stolen*, Leah."

"Have they?" she asked.

"What else could possibly have happened to them?"

She went to him and put her arms loosely around his neck. "Stop trying to make sense out of this, Stephen, and just accept that they're gone."

"But—"

"I'll miss wearing them. What woman wouldn't? They were incredible. But I don't *need* them anymore. Neither do the Gypsies. And hopefully it will be a long, long time before the pearls come to them again."

He slowly shook his head. "You're as mystical

and as mysterious as the pearls, Leah, and I love you with all my heart. Marry me, live with me, never stop loving me."

"Yes, Stephen, oh, yes."

The Gypsies danced and sang around their big campfire, their celebration lasting all night. At dawn Leah and Stephen waved good-bye to them.

"I'll miss them," she murmured, "but they'll be back."

"And we'll be here waiting for them."

"Yes, we will."

THE EDITOR'S CORNER

Next month we kick off one of LOVESWEPT's most sizzling summers! First, we bring you just what you've been asking for—

•

LOVESWEPT GOLDEN CLASSICS

•

We are ushering in this exciting program with four of the titles you've most requested by four of your most beloved authors . . .

Iris Johansen's
THE TRUSTWORTHY REDHEAD
(Originally published as LOVESWEPT #35)

•

Billie Green's
TEMPORARY ANGEL
(Originally published as LOVESWEPT #38)

Fayrene Preston's
THAT OLD FEELING
(Originally published as LOVESWEPT #45)

Kay Hooper's
SOMETHING DIFFERENT
(Originally published as LOVESWEPT #46)

•

With stunning covers—richly colored, beautifully enhanced by the golden signatures of the authors—LOVESWEPT'S GOLDEN CLASSICS are pure pleasure for those of you who missed them five years ago and exquisite "keepers" for the libraries of those who read and loved them when they were first published. Make sure your bookseller holds a set just for you or order the CLASSICS through our LOVESWEPT mail order subscription service.

And now a peek at our six new sensational romances for next month.

We start off with the phenomenal Sandra Brown's **TEMPERATURES RISING**, LOVESWEPT #336. Handsome Scout Ritland is celebrating the opening of a hotel he helped build on a lush South Pacific island when he's lured into a garden by an extraordinarily beautiful woman. But Chantal duPont has more in

(continued)

mind than a romantic interlude on this sultry moonlit night. She wants Scout all right—but to build a bridge, a bridge to connect the island on which she grew up with the mainland. Then there's an accident that Chantal never intended and that keeps Scout her bedridden patient. In the shadow of an active volcano the two discover their fierce hunger for each other . . . and the smoldering passion between them soon explodes with far-reaching consequences. This is Sandra Brown at her best in a love story to cherish. And remember—this wonderful romance is also available in a Doubleday hardcover edition.

Since bursting onto the romance scene with her enormously popular ALL'S FAIR (remember the Kissing Bandit?), Linda Cajio has delighted readers with her clever and sensual stories. Here comes an especially enchanting one, **DESPERATE MEASURES**, LOVESWEPT #337. Ellen Kitteridge is an elegant beauty who draws Joe Carlini to her as iron draws a magnet. Wild, virile, Joe pursues her relentlessly. Ellen is terrified because of her early loveless marriage to a treacherous fortune hunter. She runs from Joe, hides from him . . . but she can't escape. And Joe is determined to convince her that her shattered past has nothing to do with their thrilling future together. Linda's **DESPERATE MEASURES** will leave you breathless!

That brilliant new star of romance writing Deborah Smith gives you another thrilling story in *The Cherokee Trilogy*, **TEMPTING THE WOLF**, LOVESWEPT #338. This is the unforgettable tale of a brilliant, maverick Cherokee who was a pro football player and is now a businessman. Of most concern to Erica Gallatin, however, is his total (and threatening) masculinity. James is dangerous, perfection molded in bronze, absolutely irresistible—and he doesn't trust beautiful ''non-Indian'' women one bit! Erica is determined to get in touch with her heritage as she explores the mystery of Dove's legacy . . . and she's even more determined to subdue her mad attraction to the fierce warrior who is stealing her soul. This is a romance as heartwarming as it is heart-stopping in its intensity.

Judy Gill produces some of the most sensitive love stories we publish. In LOVESWEPT #339, **A SCENT OF ROSES,** she will once again capture your emotions with the exquisite romance of a memorable hero and heroine. Greg Miller is a race car driver who's lost his memory in an accident. His wife, Susan, puts past hurts aside when she agrees to help him recover. At his family's home in the San Juan Islands—a setting made for love—they rediscover the passion they shared . . . but can they

(continued)

compromise on the future? A thrilling story of deep passion and deep commitment nearly destroyed by misunderstanding.

It's always our greatest pleasure to discover and present a brand-new talent. Please give a warm, warm welcome to Courtney Henke, debuting next month with **CHAMELEON, LOVESWEPT** #340. This is a humorous yet emotionally touching romance we suspect you will never forget ... in large measure because of its remarkable hero. Emma Machlen is a woman with a single purpose when she invades Maxwell Morgan's domain. She's going to convince the cosmetics mogul to buy the unique fragrance her family has developed. She's utterly desperate to make the sale. But she never counts on the surprises Max will have for her, not the least of which is his incredible attractiveness. Enchanted by Emma, drawn to her against his will, Max is turned upside down by this little lady whom he *must* resist. Emma has her work cut out for her in winning over Max ... but the poor man never has a chance! An absolutely wonderful story!

And what could make for more sizzling reading than another of Helen Mittermeyer's Men of Fire? Nothing I can think of. All the passion, intensity, emotional complexity, richness, and humor you expect in one of Helen's love stories is here in **WHITE HEAT, LOVESWEPT** #341. When Pacer Dillon—that irresistible heartbreaker Helen introduced you to before—meets Colm Fitzroy, he is dead set on taking over her family business. She's dead set on stopping him. Irresistible force meets immovable object. Colm is threatened now, having been betrayed in the past, and Pacer is just the man to save her while using the sweet, hot fire of his undying love to persuade her to surrender her heart to him. Pure dynamite!

Enjoy all our LOVESWEPTs—new and old—next month! And please remember that we love to hear from you.
Sincerely,

Carolyn Nichols

Carolyn Nichols
Editor
LOVESWEPT
Bantam Books
666 Fifth Avenue
New York, NY 10103